NEW YORK REVIEW BOO
CLASSICS

THE LIMIT

ROSALIND BELBEN was born in 1941 and spent her early childhood in rural Dorset, in the southwest of England. From the age of nine she was at boarding school on the edge of Dartmoor, in Devon. Almost straight from school she went in 1959 to work for the next two years in theater, meaning to become a writer of stage plays. That didn't happen. Her subsequent life has been nomadic, her experience and employment varied—with sometimes, nevertheless, years on end passed in a single place.

The countryside of Dorset has been both inspiration and recurrent setting. Quite as much, "abroad" has exerted a powerful draw. There have been many adored destinations. Südtirol or the Alto Adige, the German-speaking Alpine region in the north of Italy, from 1978—or in the 1990s Tunisia, with its myriad Roman and Phoenician remains and Islamic culture. Many epiphanies.

In 1987 Belben was in West Berlin as a Fellow of the Artist in Residence Program, staying for fifteen months. Her novel *Our Horses in Egypt* was awarded the 2007 James Tait Black Prize for fiction. She is a Fellow of the Royal Society of Literature.

PAUL GRIFFITHS is the author of many books about Western classical music, and has written music criticism for *The Times* (London), *The New Yorker*, *The New York Times*, and other periodicals. Among his novels are *Myself and Marco Polo*, *The Lay of Sir Tristram*, and *Mr. Beethoven*, which is available from New York Review Books.

THE LIMIT

ROSALIND BELBEN

Introduction by
PAUL GRIFFITHS

NEW YORK REVIEW BOOKS

New York

THIS IS A NEW YORK REVIEW BOOK
PUBLISHED BY THE NEW YORK REVIEW OF BOOKS
207 East 32nd Street, New York, NY 10016
www.nyrb.com

First published as a New York Review Books Classic in 2023.

Library of Congress Cataloging-in-Publication Data
Names: Belben, Rosalind, 1941– author. | Griffiths, Paul, 1947 November
  24– writer of introduction.
Title: The limit / by Rosalind Belben ; introduction by Paul Griffiths.
Description: New York : New York Review Books, 2023. | Series: New York
  Review Books Classics
Identifiers: LCCN 2023012386 (print) | LCCN 2023012387 (ebook) | ISBN
  9781681377520 (paperback) | ISBN 9781681377537 (ebook)
Subjects: LCGFT: Novels.
Classification: LCC PR6052.E36 L5 2023 (print) | LCC PR6052.E36 (ebook) |
  DDC 823/.9/14—dc23/eng/20230316
LC record available at https://lccn.loc.gov/2023012386
LC ebook record available at https://lccn.loc.gov/2023012387

ISBN 978-1-68137-752-0
Available as an electronic book; ISBN 978-1-68137-753-7

Printed in the United States of America on acid-free paper.
10 9 8 7 6 5 4 3 2 1

INTRODUCTION

THE LIMIT came out in 1974 as Rosalind Belben's third book, keeping up her annual rate of production but suddenly very different. *Bogies*, in 1972, was a pair of stories dissimilar in form—one almost entirely in dialogue, the other a more regular narrative—but alike in presenting a lone female character beset. *Reuben, little hero*, the following year, had some of the qualities of both—close observation; short, broken sentences sometimes—in the context of a family story that hinged on a couple's sole child.

Difference in *The Limit* is manifold. The syntax is everywhere abrupt. Narrative time is at once stopped—at a moment, which would stand for many, when a man is sitting in the hospital room of his conspicuously older, dying wife—and exploded by scenes from both past and future. The central situation precludes dialogue to open space for interior worlds calling out to one another. Points of view (his, hers, third person) and tenses (present, past) are at once distinct and compacted. Realism is shot through with trope. The novel should fall apart; instead it falls—hurtles—together, with a clang of rightness and necessity.

Living in London from 1972 to 1978, Belben had friends who were also giving the English novel a shake, especially Giles Gordon, who became her agent as well as colleague. Dinner parties at the home he shared with his wife, Margaret, a children's book illustrator, introduced Belben to other writers. Further acquaintance in the literary world came through the publishers of *The Limit* and its predecessors, Hutchinson, for whom she read manuscripts, visiting the office weekly. Among the writers she met there was the poet-novelist Elaine Feinstein.

There was, therefore, a context for *The Limit*, but no parallel. In language and form, Belben's writing was like no other, and remains startling half a century later. The subject of the book is as old as the troubadours: the love unto death, and beyond death. But the shape that subject takes here is not pretty. Nor is it easy. Quite apart from their savage difference in age and physical condition, Anna and Ilario are separated by background and culture. She is English, from the landed gentry, he Italian, a man of the sea. Land and sea, virginity and sensuality, middle age and youth, blank white and smooth olive: these are the oppositions they—or the force of love in them—must overcome, and then time adds another, that of physical decline and robust good health, and that too is surmounted.

For this to happen, as we read, requires a driving energy in the writing—an energy that will stop at nothing, whether in charging through the norms of syntax or refusing politeness. The sympathetic reader will find the former exhilarating: a radical alterity demanded by the urgency of the storytelling.

An example. "She is perpetually worried: about green vegetables." Without that colon, the sentence would take us directly to the banal object of Anna's anxiety. With it, we are forced to stop a little, so that the perpetual worry will circle in our own minds, and the revelation of the worry's cause then have touches of humor and relief as well as bathos.

Another example. "His attention moved. Above his head, above the medicine cupboard. Perched a white enamel can." Here the irregular punctuation brings us close to a character (Ilario this time), not in confusion but in perception. Ilario's eyes jerk. The jerk is there in the separation of adverbial phrases from their verb.

As for the novel's frankness, some readers will need to be prepared for occasional unflinching encounters with bodily dysfunction or the insensitivity to animal suffering that is one aspect of English rural culture—alongside deep sympathy for dogs and horses, displayed in almost all Belben's fiction. More jarring now than it was when the novel was first published, the term "wop," derogatory slang for an Italian, is a slur Ilario would certainly have encountered in mid-twentieth-century England. From its raw moments, in another opposition, the narrative stretches to images and sentences of utter beauty and power, in much greater abundance. Wonder and distaste may even grasp each other in the one phrase.

"Without contraries is no progression," wrote William Blake in *The Marriage of Heaven and Hell*—an oppositional work in more ways than one—from which Belben takes her epigraph. Where Blake—here most particularly—engages with the Bible, Belben had a bible of her own to hand, a dictionary in which, as she records on the page opposite the epigraph, she found her chapter titles. Dictionary definitions gave her an elevated diction that would set Anna and Ilario on an eternal plane, the words defined being (with the chapters numbered here for convenience): Transmigration (1st, 15th, 19th), Rapture (2nd, 4th, 9th, 17th), Grief (3rd, 8th, 13th), Sea-Change (5th, 12th, 14th), Childhood (6th, 11th, 16th), and Future (7th, 10th, 18th). As this listing shows, the six types are distributed fairly evenly throughout the book, with the exception of the first, "The Passage of a Soul at Death into Another Body," which is brought back only after the crucial third Sea-Change—a magnificent storm scene— and then again to conclude the novel. We could never mistake, even without the evidence presented in the Future chapters, which soul is passing into which body as we turn the page after the seeming end.

Blake is by no means the only ancestor called to the stand, for joining him are English poets from Shakespeare to Stevie Smith ("Not Waving but Drowning"), never mind the unlikelihood of their being in an Italian seaman's consciousness. In Anna's, of course, they could well have been settled. Where the three Future chapters center (inevitably) on Ilario, those devoted to Childhood are Anna's, relating damage that lives on into her adult self. Though the novel disdains psychology—it states, does not explain—these chapters, in which Anna tells respectively of her mother, her father, and her blood baptism at the hunt, suggest by their vivid presence that her upbringing led irresistibly to a prolonged maidenhood and to a sudden acceptance of love only when it came from some completely other quarter. It is the expression of this love that drives into the prose to leave it in clumps and clefts through which continuity remains nevertheless strong, bounding over the obstacles of colons or even periods.

If there might be an analogy with horseback riding, this would be one element of her childhood on which Belben draws in sketching Anna's. Hence also the words of Dorset dialect, from the county in which Belben was born and raised: "brimble" (bramble), "thik" (that), and "split image," a malapropism of "spit image" (spitting image).

Tracing the author's life in this novel can, however, take

us only a very little way. *The Limit* is a work of high literary precision geared to the process of dying but also to the exultant experience of undying love. Perhaps its most autobiographical line is this, from the first Sea-Change chapter, in which Anna is observing the sun through her husband's sextant: "You are full of primitive emotion while practising an acquired scientific skill."

—PAUL GRIFFITHS

THE LIMIT

This edition
in memory of
T. D. B.

The titles of the chapters were found in
the *Hamlyn Encyclopedic World Dictionary.*

So I remain'd with him, sitting in the twisted root of an oak; he was suspended in a fungus, which hung with the head downward into the deep.

—WILLIAM BLAKE

THE PASSAGE OF A SOUL
AT DEATH INTO ANOTHER BODY

I

*isolating
one moment, one person, from the end beginning, at the beginning, finding no end, ending each hope, hoping for hope, at
the end, finishing, wishing the finish was not relative but definitive, relative not definitive, in definition, final, in finality
no longer relative, the ache for existence relating to nil, nihil-
istically unexpectant, it will not be, it is not, any longer, nothing shall happen, shall not happen thus, nothing does happen,
dust to nothing, and ashes to nothing: isolating one moment,
isolating one person*

The woman stirs: I sit at my bedside watching. Because I
cannot, there is no way in, to enter, her, she is cut off, not
with me, I not with her, I imagine it is myself. It is the nearest, that I can in memory and mind do for her. That woman
is my wife.

He sat: perfectly still, as if in a trance. But see, his eyelids
move up and down, he is blinking, a tiny flexing in his hand.
His hands are streaked like a seal's back, he is holding the
dry hair. They are together, clasped in the lap.

Ilario is a dark man, of a smooth olive. The head is black,

no strand of white, his eyeballs round and brown. Everything about him has this colour olive, it is throughout Ilario, one colour; his skin is soft. Ilario is a handsome person. The person over there he stares at is not handsome. The ugly person in the bed is this man's wife.

Ilario caught the faint mutter, waited. It came to—nothing. The small tenseness, which it had aroused, vanished.

Anna was concerned with identity, the last important item of life to remember. I am Anna. I most urgently am I. My name is: a frown, a choke, a treetrunk falls heavily over the mind. A stammer, a look of imperceptible anguish: my name is Anna   : the family name essential even now. She cannot recall it, mercifully supposes she's said it—name of her marriage, her husband, Ilario—and subsides.

His feet remain, patient. The shoes were canvas, socks blue, trousers brown, shirt wide open at the throat—a picture of the uncomplicated man. His clothes aren't specially suitable: who cares? Does she see what he's wearing, that it differs not a jot from her calico gown? Inwardly Ilario groaned.

The woman lay utterly silent. He wished she could acknowledge his abiding presence. Anna was beyond all recognition.

The pain began with a piercing whistle in her ears, pouring like molten lead into her brain, the part of her inside the skull, the heart of her: the soul, swimming to bob below a lid, the lid clamped vigorously upon incipient eruption until the last moment, until the end, where so many torments would have to go. Remove the lid of my skull, Ilario she knew was there, who was he, his voice his breath his hands were a person she recognised, accepted as her loved: remove the lid of my skull, she pleaded, allow the pain I feel to overflow. Then it loosed itself from her, so she was outside it, could hand it to the man between the bed and the chair on which he perched, taut as a bird. Take this, she said, pass this pain. I to thee Ilario. Has he come? retrieved softly in the mouth? Leave—leave plumly at the feet of my ice. Her toes were frozen extremities. First warm my feet, do not permit me to go in pieces, a cheshire cat. Hold my toes, keep them here, retain them o my love, drop anchor for my feet. I do not want to perish. She touched the forehead with her red hot fingertips, crooked the bones of her fingers round an empty chin. He stood swiftly, bent, and called her name. There was no reaction or response. At the tepid smile he has often wept.

To her it seemed interminable: I have a job, my job is departure, I need to get on, I am not doing it well. If I concentrate harder, powerfully try... And the pain swept again blotting deliberate thought to the point in which she said let us leave each other, I can tolerate togetherness no longer, or she screamed, without making a sound anyone else could hear.

He coughed briefly, was quite quiet. She turned her eyes. Ilario did not credit them with sight. She is, by the length of her, tall, and verily thin. Her shanks, in a foetal gesture, clap skin to skin, flesh to flesh from bald pubis down insubstantial thighs to joints resembling knees, ankles. On the rib cage, her chest, nipples of limp breasts slide, erotic antitheses. In the creased belly the colon, blessedly void, historic battleground of desperate remedies. At the base of her neck, a shallow palpitation. The hair of her head is cropped to two centimetres, sparse, and grey. Features come into focus, and fade. Visible and invisible. Sharp nose, pale eyes, their blue washed away. Out of the chin grow whiskers, the upper lip yields a forest: evil flourish, a hormonal disorder: must it matter? Partly man, man or woman, woman or man, or both: in the end aren't they identical. But she's old, old surely enough to be his mother, old more than illness ages: why is this legless lady *ancient*? She is Ilario's wife. She gave him twenty years, people commented unkindly. A strong body, a strong will: for six weeks she refused sustenance, for six days she spits water over the sheet: a rational attempt to destroy resources? To all intents and purposes nearly comatose, she conceives an act of will?

The ice cream has come. I prepare to administer ice cream to my wife. Sit up a little, Anna. I try to grip the shoulders to haul her out of the pillow. The lips and tongue haven't noticed the ice cream yet, they don't know about it. She keeps eternally an inner strength, she lies twisted in the best position. And I am rather helpless. He shrugs, tears in his eyes. He wraps a big bath towel and some paper under her face. The wrong angle. He dips a cheap metal spoon into the dish, conveys one mouthful to her lips, touches the lips with the spoon and with ice cream he taps her teeth. The rest is reflex. Almost automatic—extending her tongue, chewing—an obvious sense of wonderment—the enormous problematical swallow. Almost automatic. How, he thinks, changeable are the desires of these lips and these teeth that one day one hour one minute decide ice cream to be unwanted, on no account to be sent to the gullet and stomach, and now do open and shut in mute invitation like a suffocating fish. Anna's eyes were closed and the ice cream ran from the corners of her mouth. A simple food to cool the hurt in her mind—the lemon, squeezed in one small pause between bouts. It is finished, the mouth still hopeful. I wipe the mouth, to indicate an end. But Anna's lips part, her tongue hangs out red and clean. Should I procure a (difficult) second helping? I wet the towel instead, dab at the glum lips: which retreat, sinking into the pillow. I find grease for sore lips. I apply it. The creature rolls her lips, uncannily precise. He washes his hands with obsessive caution, denying his distaste. Ilario writes on her chart the hour of the day, adding: ice cream. Then again, he takes his seat, his original position. Presently she will go purple. The catheter tube stirs, he sees incredible liquid pass his objective eye. He might, at the window, observe reality in distant motion. Far beneath them, people crossed courtyards, dodged traffic in the road. Further, the flat belonging to her brother where he sometimes slept, an uncomfortable visitor, never forgiven for being a wop. Reality was here: suspended in hospital and indefinite. He recognised the banality of his situation: for her, the uniqueness, the only one. It was, he was she, she was he, he breathed her foetid air, she drained his prevailing health, his brownness from the sea.

She is pondering: who am I? what is my name? this man will speak my name for me, he knows who I am, he knows. And she clung to the cotton pillow, gripped it as if she feared its loss. A valued acquisition. Lying in a strange bed, trying hard to go.

Nurses arrive to turn her. Ilario abandons Anna. He leaves the room. For intimacies it is best each intimate witnesseth not the other. He whose sperm penetrates the emaciated body may not watch the secret ministrations, but stifle, merely, wallowing, in the astonishing stink of the cream they smear between her legs. She shouts and yells. A clear voice, grumbling, cantankerous. Any old woman in a wheelchair, alert and alive. She fights, rejecting out of hand a drink. Politely they prod her cheeks, utter that name, thrust the drinking cup through clenched teeth. She forgets the ice cream has made her thirsty: she cannot really connect. Ilario listens to the girls laughing. Anticipating the faithful man whose devotion endears him to them, they place the chair on the other side of the bed. When he returns he will sit at once and see her face.

Pouting, she lies as if fallen from a great height.

She has been disturbed, and begins to talk. This goes on for ever.

The words swam round Ilario's head, the stillness of him, in, in, in, she cries, loudly, urgently, with the most longing. In the middle of confusion, a massive bleed in her brain, she is able to grasp the fact of her dying. She knows: what she is doing. Not in a fatal helpless sense. But positive. Deliberate. Like walking to the noose. She places foot after foot towards the gallows, wide open her eyes, her nose as straight as a dog. Ilario, absorbed in the moment of dreadful compassion, does not understand the metaphor: heaven. She is saying: in. In. As we live by metaphors so we die. He does not understand yet, and is saddened. Drowning in the pathos, he feels his own hot tears.

THE CARRYING OF A PERSON
TO ANOTHER PLACE OR SPHERE
OF EXISTENCE

I

The wedding night, the marital bed. The beginning before the end.

Ilario blushed scarlet for his bride.

Our honeymoon we spent in England, the words we spoke were English. My wife personified all those things I thought most English. I loved her.

An iron maiden. Forged in a landscape of snow, for this was the English winter of 1962. Set in a sea of blue snow, frozen, buried there. I groped, to discover and retrieve her body: I drove a long stake into her heart, fumbling clumsily about upon the surface of her soul. The spirit leaked from my lips, but she did not melt. She turned into a pillar of salt, I became simply stone. Jack Frost touched both countryside and compassion. And in the valleys I know snow lies deepest, concealing treacherous cracks, fissures to trap my willing flesh. I stare. Anna was unaware of my regard, because she had closed her eyes, expecting the misery of exposure to transport her to sudden ecstasy, how else could it be. Alarmed, she has surrendered modesty. Madonna. She trusted me. Anticipated me. Stricken, I dressed her in a white nightgown. In her mind's eye she sees not love, she is remembering the act of mating animals. Suspended below her brain a safety net contains images of bulls copulating, stallions in flagrante delicto, and dogs, even birds, squirrels, or rats.

The silence scorched me.

Perhaps a lifetime would pass away. She died. I died. I had not observed the phenomenon in any other woman. Anna hung protruding like a male.

She was also forty, a virgin, and too narrow.

He despaired of ever penetrating her distorted organ.

A whole week in a wilderness of grief.

Or: in the New Forest, not far from Brockenhurst.

Stalking fallow deer by day, while at night I stuffed one finger, one finger only, up her incredible cunt. Innocently I ran across a hare in the road: it added acrimony to our wounds. I dreamt, when I slept, badly. I conceived a bright idea: but it confused her and she shrank. Anna glued her face to the sheet. Mentally she separated me from my cock. Otherwise I caused her injury the real man could not possibly have desired. And then, when she'd grown accustomed to the sight of naked me, she ogled my body. Convulsed in raucous laughter. A crescendo of embarrassment. I felt menaced by so many conflicting emotions. Sheer anger made me sweat: although the weather outside continued cold, racked upon the bed our skins stuck together, issuing crude sucking noises. Yes, the sweat was mine: your skin, I remember, remained dry. Unattractive. However, above the waist she functioned quite well. Touch the breasts—piping hot. Tickle the toes—each a tiny iceberg. Clearly defined limits of responsive flesh. Ah, but she thought me obscene, the dimensions of her new experience overwhelming. A dull crimson suffused the room: a sunset, merely, against its window panes.

And you: at arm's length, the puzzling duty. I wrapped

her fingers—those stiff, skeletal digits—around the penis: makeshift I moved the two of us. About to concede contamination by the fruits of carnal knowledge, she howled: Ilario, you are hurting my *hand*. The polite Italian catches sperm in his handkerchief. Mortifying his wife. I tried to explain: between your legs you are too little (never mind the rest): your *fica*, she is aged eleven. Had she brought him to a false altar, to the sure contempt of chambermaids?

She leads him through the forest, she appears incapable of walking behind anyone and from now on she will take every chance to reverse their roles. On the seventh day she removes her fur glove to pat a pony's nose. I journeyed to Brockenhurst determined to fuck the woman with me: thanks to that ugly old mare I did. Are you happy? she asked, pretending untroubled bliss. To my own astonishment I was. I'd accepted with painful speed the mutation. And the honeymoon, at least, came to a conclusion.

The degree of his regret seemed out of all proportion to the event.

A CAUSE OR OCCASION OF
KEEN DISTRESS OR SORROW

I

Ilario watched Anna waiting to die.

For months on end he is forced to sit beside a person whom he loves—very much—whose poor head must be filled with thoughts, and images, of death.

The inclination of her body (the declination of the sun) indicates the direction and position of her mind.

If she pushes the chin forward aggressively, blinks, frowns, touches her legs saying look my circulation has stopped, I can feel certain she is thinking about herself. But if she lets the body droop or paradoxically drives those weak pins to walk—absently shading a face swathed in scarves from an unkind wind—I know her most pressing preoccupation has gone away.

Food became a special comfort. Although there were many things she couldn't eat, without making her indigestion. Worse, the liver bad. I brought trays for the knees.

Anna picks her knife and fork from the plate and waves them in the air, a baby eating. I tuck a napkin—her bib—into the slack collar. She examines her pale fatless portion avidly. Already salivating, masticating. La bocca famished, craving sensual dummies thrust between its oozy lips. Pleasure accumulates: some of the stuff going in falls out. Consumable objects, wrapped by cracked parchment: an orifice indeed.

Potatoes: no butter. Yellow pears: no cream. Spinach: for the inside. Carrots, fish, apples. Tea, no coffee.

Ah: Anna is heaving her carcass to the kitchen, a mighty trek, in an injured silence. I've forgotten the salt, she fancies sauce. Once there she will gobble groceries in the imagination.

And in memory, too, food was important. She desired nursery dishes—rice pudding, macaroni cheese, semolina syrup, baked eggs, junket: strange inglesi concoctions eaten with Nannie, recalled so nostalgically.

Cheese and eggs are taboo.

In our local health store I discover barley kernels, she's thrilled. I humour her passion, tracking flavours of the whole world, most are quite unsuitable. The diseased stomach won't tolerate her last whims. She has to manage on marge. Glucose protects the old liver. She is perpetually worried: about green vegetables.

Always her body was thin, tall but thin. Now Anna possesses a belly, she rests two hands over it pointing her attention at the television. Never again shall I see a horse racing on television and not remember those afternoons. We give humble heartfelt thanks for this thy box. The belly she carries looks like a child.

The woman appears lopsided: if she lies in the bath—after showers at sea a welcome luxury—and we regard her body yellow, water laps on an uneven shore, the curves of this female island grow uncanny, the mound rising distended, midst a sea of troubles, while other bits waste wrinkled into it. Only...a jaundiced glitter caused the...tummy to...

shine. She places some fig-leaf flannel over the indecency, she balances sponges, soap, ducks, and boats. . . .

For suffering and dying she's an animal: she goes to earth, to her lair, to lie in the dark, to lick her wounds. She has come home. She may love the sea but it is to our own home she wants to retreat. She must anyway, at least she wishes it. We had arrived home, harbouring our illnesses. She expected me to leave, I oppressed her, my presence obviously necessary. You were unfair, she said, one needs a philosophy, to cope. Anna did cope. I did not.

They told her. Your malignancy remains, couldn't all be extracted, found entwined in awkward places, will respond to alternative treatment.

A shock, yes. She was sad. She was sorry. She polished favourite furniture lovingly using elbow grease for tears and beeswax for balm. Or she anointed the fine wood in vinegar. I still smell the acrid scent seeping through the rooms of our empty house. Long afterwards, or long ago. To forget, to forget.

Objects we neglect suddenly have exquisite value. She touched each precious possession, laid hands upon, blessed these blind and soulless creatures as if like dogs they also breathed. She catechised me, gathering panic. It's apparently important, vital. That I recognise rarities, first editions, illustrations by Dulac, the best silver, china, ornaments, glass. To preserve indefinitely her sentiment stuffed, bolstered. Your dearest Swinburne shall marry my sextant, I swear it. But, listening, I'm bemused and deeply shaken by the macabre inventory. Delving, sifting, exclaiming, she dwells over the detail of her life while denying the supposition of her death. She is determined to survive.

To change, not merely adapting but bringing about a future. She insists, the bedroom must be pale mauve, a colour from her menstrual rainbow: I obey, decorate, my sleep made consequently hideous, I think she's happy. Odd jobs don't amuse me, I try to obliterate mauve in my mind, failing. Terribly, I hate these shades of purple (blood).

The bride peers through windows in her lavender bower and sees a pink wishbone charging across the sky to the west from the east. Towards the faraway trees. Certain whatever she wishes will come true, she struggles only with the choice— happiness or health. Time reduced itself, distance shortened, Anna chose happiness, the cloud vanished.

Clouds do occur. She had arrived at natural phenomena. And in the night sky Orion remained becalmed, or upon it pinioned in painful clarity. The most loved constellation. Her stars shining, for her agony. Twinkle. O Sirius the dog. She searches them and smiles. Perception sharpened by the surgeon's knife.

In the garden, she held pebbles the size of giant pills in the palms of her trembling hands: weeding the flower beds being an excuse not to swallow them. She was awfully bad at swallowing pills. If the pills had all been green she would have swallowed the lot quite easily. But they were pasty faced. They were white. Unable to bend, she squatted on a sketching stool, grovelling amongst our fair earth.

Or earthwards she lowered the body, examining the insects thereof: ignoring worms. She loved centipedes, ants, and beetles. Miraculous grasshoppers she truly adored. She touched her lips with daffodils. The buddleia cast a complex shadow across Anna's face.

The garden leads us to water, the nearby river to the distant sea. This unattainable ocean.

Beside a worn groin on a sandy beach she remarks: please, Ilario, bury me at sea. Please.

If something happened to me, said she, supposing that one day something will happen to me, I'd like you to know what it is you must do.

I believe it has to be ashes: will you inquire.

And then. Begging me not to burn her. I was in tears, the expedition overwhelmed me. We stood surrounded by broken deckchairs, broken buckets, broken sandcastles—everything seemed ruined—below an absurd pier: a cold spring evening at the seaside caused my imagination to go berserk.

God had been disposed of long ago.

Neither she nor I acknowledged the divinity. Our faith lay in mankind, not in its mythical maker. She showed little sign of abdicating conviction for a god she spent her life denying. We agreed upon the possibility of a different reality: but that did not leave Anna any *hope*.

However, relations were reviewed, like the fleet. Six remaining sisters received us with sadness. Richard and his household, the hated Maxwell, treated her to impassive embarrassment. Perhaps it was phlegm.

Later, her head ached and her ear hurt piercingly.

She made me strange accusations: she told me I was weak. The master's ticket I owed to my wife, my navigation having grown terrible. She pulled my strings, she smoothed my path. She is father of the man. Without a wife, without her, I am nothing, I am useless. Was always useless.

She: injured me. More than I can say.

Then suddenly it finished. All, all over. She abandoned the fetishist objects, she lost interest in the birds, plants, animals. Water, fire, and air had no meaning. She turned inwards. She turned on herself. She forgot me, absolved me by dividing us. I stayed on the outside looking in: she became absorbed, her existence absolute. I am sure Anna perceived no greater reality than her own being. The necessary. The important. She, and she alone, mattered. She had already departed from me. I could hardly follow. She couldn't take me. On her night journey of no return. I think she must have known.

And Ilario? He thinks: I too am dying. Haunted by an obsessive image, he awaits his imminent end, not as calmly as his wife.

THE CARRYING OF A PERSON
TO ANOTHER PLACE OR SPHERE
OF EXISTENCE

2

There was once a day, there is always one day impossible to rub from the memory. It began, it begins and ends innocently. Through the door to our bathroom. The door is unlocked, Anna has forgotten that this time she really wished to lock it. Startled, she glared at me with a face of horror. He said mildly, I'm early, my ETA must have been a bit out. But she could not smile. Her attitude the shape of an ape. An animal. The body curved, had no focus in my eyes, seemed disjointed. Her arms hung from the shoulders, they were very long, even longer than usual. The jaw protuberant, the expression beneath these anthropoidal brows inhuman, unhuman. An old skinny baboon. Or, as you're so heavily whiskered, the orang-outang. The sinews, the swellings, the fat and the thin: all abnormally proportionless. The utter ugliness of Anna: caught, her trousers down. Go away, she implored me. I hadn't realised she possessed the gift of speech. He stood transfixed while water escaped some apparatus she was holding in her hands and dripped quietly onto the floor. He felt uncertain, unable to grasp the complete picture. The articles of washing, shaving, shampooing were familiar. Also, the sophisticated smell, their cleansing power, and wholesomeness. The bathmat had slipped, crumpled, lay askew. Sponges lived, breathed, were watching him. His attention moved. Above his head, above the medicine cupboard. Perched a white enamel can. Actually, it is precariously balanced. Out of its spout came red rubber. A hose which dangled, then curled, to disappear into the place where she fumbled at least to turn off the tap. To stop what was still pouring up her. Still switched to her intestinal system. Anna looks extremely flushed. Are you embarrassed. She straddled the lavatory. Her knickers had got wet, and trodden on. Insanity. Imbecile. Ma cosa fai? Does your position standing mitigate humiliation. She admits to lie flat is to increase the pressure. To lower that container eases it. Upright, she finds she works best. Better. Madonna. Hotter water too, inflamed blood, intoxicated brains. The loo, she says shyly, takes care of everything. Allora, dai, dai. He strikes a note sarcastic. She is a novelty. Don't we share and see and know about each other: everything. Yes yes. Perhaps ten minutes pass. We regard the pocks, the veins in her thighs. She has been riddled since her menopause with sore spots and much chagrin. Our change of life, change of: what? When the piss belched, and she peed alarmingly as I entered her, the ultimate disconcertment, or the blood in great purple dobs unexpectedly dirtied the bed and I would wake, entangled, Anna's inside matted on my own hair. Now she's grotesque. The scene, like so many, is skewered in my mind. Impaled. Stuck through and through: or I am. Triumphant, she interferes artificially with herself, therefore perceives no obscenity. She touches the black plastic nozzle. You can't understand, said my wife. She supposed me to enjoy physical perfection. I am the only angel here, sound in wind and limb: blessed by the gods. I'm *lucky*. But I clutch at the door, causing a draught. She grimaces, fingering goose flesh, breaking out in a sweat, reeling against the bath edge. Oh the red red rubber perisheth. Boots the Chemist fecit. You keep the box hidden. Out of my sight. She thinks I wouldn't like it, why? We are both ashamed. The bathroom for Anna seems a trap: I was already aware of it as a cage. And then we wait. As we have, over the years, constantly waited. As they will, in time to come, continue waiting. Before she is able to hold on no longer and abruptly squats. He was shaken by the strength of his response to the situation. If emotion could be purely visual, this tortured me.

And how we have ached to make love while she's healing from the laparotomy (a surgical incision *through* the flank or loin, any incision into any part of the abdominal wall, to establish the diagnosis) to discover the extent of its parasitical activity. It so happens I have never previously copulated with a pregnant woman. I adapt: my body to her mound, I take the two of them (the ovary on the left, the sinister, unwilling to start an honest infant—indeed, incapable—having spawned malignancy) kissing her sickly flesh. She lifts me: swollen upon my pet balloon, I have all my parts in the air: Anna is my ground earth, a putrid bog I poke at with my drooling cazzo: inflated, she is meanwhile in great pain. It was his weight she wanted to feel, to be beaten, flattened, crucified underneath (he said: you're mistaken, could this be where you go wrong?) and she bore him on her belly, in incredible affliction. She, good Christ, desired it, not I. She pointed, pressed, indicated the place. Saying, I am tender, I am not quite *right*, here. Here. As if by admitting discomfort she has accepted recovery. Though she's hardly in a fit state to notice the balm.

Years ago: she pleaded, hurt me. The next logical step was, then, to damage deliberately, and loving her, to injure, to suspend hateful compassion. More than the teeth bite, more than the nails scratch, the fingers pinch. Twist and deform her. I recoiled: the words alone were enough to make frenzy in my head. Our bodies were tired and sore, sliding up and down the rough sheets as the ship tossed, and pitched. She provoked me, to measure the total of her sex.

Now, her shin rasps against his thigh. He extends his arm, his hand, embracing the shiny ill knee of his elderly invalid. He rubbed and soothed it. He ran his hand from the ankle to the crutch, hugged the leg to his side. He feels the coarseness, she has shaved, yet she has great difficulty in bending: her hair sprouts fiercely. She straightens her knees. Out of doors, it is raining hard. Frantic, we are at least coupled.

Consume me, she weeps, my disease, my foul breath, my yellow tongue, my sweat, remove it and return me to happiness, cure me of my wounds, raise me to another place—tell me, why does that peace pass all understanding? Let me see reasons, *reasons*: I should not be then so *lost*. In my tummy, acute PAIN. In my cunt the texture of his penis. I am exhausted. Vieni. And very simply, he comes.

Have I not, in moments past, lain my bursting member alongside some mocking imitation through the thin divide, Anna like an egg-bound hen clucking her dismay. Or put fingers up her, traced in a kind of rapt disgust and with my love for her complete, the contours and encrustations of misery? Anna abject, hiding her face in the pillow, soaking it in endless anguish. She finds crudity intolerable. Obsessed by her crudity, not mine. The hair on my legs, stiff, as a man's is: and I nod, smiling. Black growing between my breasts: I stroke her there. The hair of my crutch arrives at my knees. A beard decorates my chin. The pills, he protested, feebly. Isn't my voice: deep? He shrugs. And my skin, how is that. You are silly, amore, he said, loathing the self-pity. The savagery. Why is his skin always brown and clean and sweet to the taste. Why is she ill? There's no answer, not one which would satisfy her: instead, he kisses her. Mouth cheeks eyes hair, touching her throat, he gripped her scraggy shoulders and shook: Anna, oh Anna. She was drenched in tears, and uncomforted. It's Ilario for whom she weeps. Leaving him. I laid a hand over her tummy but could not contain the tumour.

At their heads they lie apart, joined below yet forced on the pillow just to stare at each other. Siamese twins.

In the bathroom Anna coils the rubber round her hand. She stuffs this into the little can. She adds the black plastic tap. She also stinks. Is it essential? he asked her. She bites her lip, chews it. Mumbles reproaches. She appears to be hurt by something.

I long to crawl away and be most violently sick. But I stand up and kiss her.

A CHANGE
BROUGHT ABOUT BY THE SEA

I

Anna in hospital played the records from her memory. She leant her head against a hard pillow, longing to shut her eyes. In a door to a peeling balustrade the glass seemed to quiver. In the glass, as it moved, the sun's image was perfectly captured. The sun, paler than the moon. Bereft. Bereft of its power, and of its magnitude. No glare, no dazzle, no blinding light. The breeze touched the door, the sun became double. Two and two make one, one and one make two. In the surgical ward's french window. The sun separates, the door swings, the sun merges making one sun, the sun which is reality, the real sun. But creating the illusion of two. Anna focused greedily her eyes upon this odd phenomenon. Comforted, the sun she saw there was the sun at noon. At its zenith. As if through the smoky little glasses of a sextant. She recalled the intense pleasure of reducing the sun to a personal horizon. Taking a sun sight—a simple enough task—involved an element of human will, her will. I, actually I, cause the sun to fall, to drop out of the sky. You waggle your fingers and wave it down. You sit the sun tenderly on the absolute edge of your visual world. You may, if you wish, push it into the sea. Or dance it about on distant cloud banks. On your command, it tilts across the heavens at alarming

speed. You have drawn the sun's sting. You are full of primitive emotion while practising an acquired scientific skill.
Anna chuckled aloud: the trolley lady beamed: Anna clutched
the cup of tea murmuring thank you: like a docile child.
Then she did shut her eyes. Supposing. I am in my leper
colony. A place I visit many times in dreams. My waking
and sleeping dreams. By the Bay of Benin I swear I shall not
forget it. Ilario and Anna pack their picnic for another inland
journey. North from Abidjan. North from Abidjan we discover no ordinary African village. Tourists, snoopers, uncertain of our true identity. Curiosity not philanthropy
drives us to it and our thirst for oddity will for ever be as-
suaged. A rocky hill, a *gate*, a greasy pole, a limp flag: these
I remember. The huts of concrete and corrugated. And drains
channelled through concrete. Earth has more charm and
cleansing properties but concrete sluices very nicely. The
village mountainous, chilly in the interminable drizzle before
the rains, without wind. All is quite quiet, all is still. Are
those kids pot bellied refugees from the land of the rising
sun: no. Too far. Too strange, this land. Not our land, so
why have we come. A blind man squats, turning his thumb.
A woman sinks her nails into a young girl's hair. Many
people are stiff, most are crippled, but to begin with they
appear normal: why, then, have we begun to inspect them.
Silently we stare as total strangers at one another. Ilario digs
in his pocket, he produces dash and starts things moving:
he is putting a coin in their slot, the mechanical tableau
grinds into action. A responsible person will be fetched. A
child, we notice, has few toes. A strapping male, chunks of
the body missing. In the dust, a dozen thin fowls stampede
a beetle passing. The responsible person arrives. He exclaims:
oh we are delighted to welcome visitors. No one comes dur-

ing six months. That's a long time. The town doctor refuses, you see. We don't, immediately, see. Missionary boss on leave seeking funds. In France. By the way, I am Marie-Paul. We shake hands with him, he with us. Anna and Ilario and Marie-Paul share some intelligence, amiability. A gratifying rapport. May I show you our dying man. It is agreed. The man dying lies in the hospital, a harsh square of concrete at the heart of the complex. He's in pain. And Marie-Paul regrets showing us a chap dying and in pain, he regrets also the pain, for the man's sake. The chap dies atop an enormously tall bed clad in only a pair of khaki shorts. The khaki shorts conceal little of his advanced emaciation. Marie-Paul promptly reads our thoughts: a drought of medicines, verily a dire lack. A perfunctory shrug. Please, permit me to exhibit the vegetable garden of Monsieur Lambert. The absent French-man had surrounded his bungalow in concentric rows. Ilario admires the flowers. I the turnips. Fortifications. His moat. A lonely man. Is Monsieur married? Non, la femme c'est nous. Marie-Paul, on tiptoe, a finger to the lips, beckons us to the drawing room window. A deserted room. Your noble missionary must feel loneliness. The sole European, for miles and miles and miles: it matters? Well, he needed to set the bungalow apart from you. To return to his life's work we follow labyrinthine paths. Wondering about him, or just wondering. Why is the dying man dying, and of what does he die, and so on? Of leprosy, what else. Here we boast ac-commodation to house thirty families, here is my quarter, here you see my scowling wife suspecting sudden photogra-phy. Any children? we ask. Laughter. Umpteen miscarriages. Ah. Ah. Anna did not bear progeny either. Nor tried even, and failed. Treatment can be obtained. Cash buys a beauti-ful treatment. Ilario offers a donation. We have, after all's said and done, looked at a lot of lepers. And Anna in bed sipped her tea. Burble burble. Burble burble. The dying man duly died. No doubt. At my own expiry I shall cease too. They ran towards ill Anna as the cup tipped over and the tea spilt and the saucer shattered when it hit the floor. Scalded her lap, poor old body, uttered a friendly soul. Never mind, dear. I mind because I cannot order my dreams. Always, always, my stars were elusive, fragile. I may castigate the sun for promiscuity; I deeply love my favourite stars. Fomalhaut, Vega, Capella, Polaris, Jupiter. Venus, Regulus, Arcturus. Ilario's passion for the sea. If I possess a philosophy to die with it is this: nothing means more to me than the things of the natural world, yet they are nothing to me in death. I do not recognise any spiritual quality: a fish is a fish, a daffodil is a flower, a splendid animal is simply better made, chemically, than I am. Sunset, dawn, twilight, the noise of vast water—these are good memories in my brain. By the time I die they are already gone. My husband Ilario is part of memory. The meaning of I is left to me. No one has helped me, no one has changed me, I believe in nothing but myself. Nor shall our love transcend death. At my expiry I *will* cease. Nurse, we women who have been cut up feel cold: you must shut our windows. She was fiercely protective of her fellow bedridden—do you care about them, he said, or merely their rights. Ilario doesn't sympathise, his concern encompasses her alone: the rest seem unfortunate superfluities. You are narrow, she aggressively asserted, your mentality one track. Perhaps the landlocked husband should go back to sea. Visiting time looms. Ironically, one natural spectacle was denied her. The sight of it is given to many. In fact to most of us. Across every ocean—surely another world—the sun, setting on a fine day, flashes green, at the precise moment it sinks. The green flash is an illusion of nature. Ability to witness it misses Anna out. Though her eyes are as keen as any eyes. A curious epitome of her tragedy. You appear at the end of my bed. Desperately she inflicts love upon him. Barriers lowered. Defences naked. And ashamed. Conscious, in full control of her faculties, but weakened by constant exposure to inclement hospital weather. Day dreaming makes the time fly. Anna drinks water, chokes gently. She'll be fast asleep before I reach her. However, she did come home on Thursday.

THE STATE OF TIME
OF BEING A CHILD

I

Protect me from my mother. Make my father beloved come alive. Rise: my dog from the dead. But prayers are seldom if ever answered. Anna is born in 1922 (twenty years will pass before his birth): childhood proves unsatisfactory, an unsalutary experience: and to it the Anna grown up is irreversibly linked, to it pieces of her now are related: they are parts of her score yet do not, repeat not, determine her whole works. Simply, her machinery lacked oil in the past. I hate my mother. As I have not hated any human being then or now, or ever shall hate as much again.

My dog is killing a cat. It is horrible, horrible. I am aged fourteen, the dog three. The years of the cat unknown. Anna and the dog are tearing the cat apart, she to save, he to destroy: she is anaemic, he is at his prime. Witness the despair of this marmalade cat. It was lying in long grass, oh foolishly. The cat has precognition: the moment when it realises death will shortly follow is written across its small face, saturated in blood. Dark and wet, metamorphosed into a rat, it pisses on Anna. The dog has got it by the guts.

One sister's ears were stuck with plaster to her head. Another ate bananas on a sofa, never speaking. Innocent sisters: their rare red frocks stain the armpits crimson, the colour of the curse, they imagine they've begun it: or tumbling on the croquet lawn with a very foreign bird, a visiting male child, suppose themselves impregnated.

The dog has got it by the guts. His good teeth squash the poor cat's guts. That must be why the cat is going to die presently. The dog seems inept at killing a cat. Anna puts her hands into the dog's mouth. Twisting, the brave pussy bites the dog's lips and Anna's hands. It claws the bad dog, and the hands, and the arms. There's no sting to be felt yet. Anna and the cat are slithering in doggy saliva, white and frothy. Of the three of us, only two will continue to exist.

And here they all are, except Richard, having no education. Because Mum's temper couldn't be controlled, each successive governess departed before the Roman invasion. Anna, deep in Gibbon, hoped her thoughts might drift in the right direction. Dad, although erudite and witty, restricted his wit and erudition to the issue of epigrams constantly during dinner. Richard was sent to Cheltenham, which was chilly.

Of the three of us, only two will continue to exist. I shout at him, he's listening to the sound, of the cat's blood beating. So he drags Anna, who is hanging on to him, through the grass: she loses a shoe, scrapes a knee, scalps a knuckle. Because she loves him and he loves her she can touch his tongue, his purple throat: he falters, dropping the cat. He peers at Anna between his legs. The cat crawls convulsively, not a mile but a yard: Anna and the dog watch while, gasping, the cat expires.

The mother's proverbial passion caused her to make and break many dearest friendships. She had a rude and violent nature. She composed poetry. Later, she drank. She died pickled in brandy. She greatly disliked the idea of death. But she was doomed to misunderstanding life and to being misunderstood always, always. Her own worst enemy, said Nannie. Often the origin of remarks. Nannie endured Mum by ignoring her and carrying on regardless. This was a thing Nannies did well. Old Nannie is the person Anna prefers, or may it be: the dog.

No one will accuse Anna of moral cowardice transporting the cat's corpse to the drawing room. I'm sure it's wrong to be yellow. It was a tom and has made Anna stink. Blood sticks to her hair—the dog's blood, from his tongue torn by the cat. The dead cat seems unsuitable indoors: the intestines fall about rather.

There Dad is in his bookroom. He has a young lad sitting with him, an attentive ear. Dad's fawning sycophants provide us with chronic irritation. He gives his time to them not us. They are extremely pretty.

Cats disappeared like vermin and increased every day. Cats were exterminated, strangled, poisoned, and hanged. These cats have run wild for generations. In name they belong to the mother. I swear I'll leave one in a bush if it happens again. It won't happen again. Mum has flown off the handle, breathing fire.

The worm turned and Richard goes, never to return.

I am estranged from her, hopelessly.

Outside, Anna's dog cringed on the ground. Her scratches decorate her arms in orange.

Dad spent his wedding night in tears.

She suggested burial of the victim. But no.

Punishments flowed profusely.

At seventeen Anna can read, write, and ride. She rides well. Dashingly. Home is unbearable. Dad is no longer part of the picture. Spirited, she tries to escape. Travelling in a railway train.

Reaching Nannie, she was almost howling.

They forced Richard to regurgitate his sister from London. Anna, tossed contemptuously back towards childhood, finds the dog she abandoned stone cold dead.

An eye for an eye.

Soon the war will come.

She shut him in a stable to lick his wounds on a bed of clean straw. The beating was too late. It is all too late.

1939 spells freedom.

Nannie grows prickles on her face.

He stirs uneasily in the dark, my strange, intense boy.

I shall never cry.

Shot through the heart.

TIME THAT IS TO BE
OR COME HEREAFTER

I

Because the passenger was English Ilario invited her to his own table. But as she knew some Italian they spoke mostly in that language. She understood well, replied haltingly. Ilario had forgotten the English which once was so fluent in a blotting out from his mind of his English marriage. Yet that marriage possessed him. And he felt very lonely. E molto simpatica, lei: he said. And he meant it. Their conversations, extremely intimate, are conducted with grammatical formality. Her ear is excellent, she will remember the voyage for his slipshod Neapolitan accent.

The others, the other passengers, welcomed her. Then, watching the prolonged muttering, the obvious confidences between a neurotic captain and the solitary girl, they became hostile, antagonistic, aggressive, they cold-shouldered her convinced she slept in his bed: she did not. A love making later could only be the outcome of tortured intense discussion. The empathy seemed strange and immediate.

He observed her taking leave of New York in the heat where water swirled past knotted with contraceptives like crude pack ice. The Hudson River, an obscene, perfectly opaque, and human sewer. Two men kissed her goodbye at the dockside. Ilario has a bird's eye view. One man accompanies her on board. In her small cabin they screw. And she tells him: why? asks Ilario, must you spill the beans. She laughed. The gangway springs, has a weak rail, holes to fall through. She wears levis and a flimsy T-shirt. Her luggage was a scrubbed white sea-bag handsewn by the lover. His friend a mere acquaintance. Ilario recognises her blank emotion, perceiving identical faces of Anna. Absurdly comforted himself, he longs to comfort this familiar manifestation of female grief.

Her hair: it is so short (Anna's, as she died). Hair (also) of darkest brown. Eyes: they stare clear and sharp. Direct eyes. And the breasts of a child (Anna's in middle age, middle life, near the end of life, at the end, the finish).

She approached, and the American too. We were loading all three forward hatches. A vast black fellow stood by the nearest winch, roaring. The longshoremen gesticulate laconically. The painting cradle creaked beneath the port bow. The bosun bent to light his cheap cigarette. I have little curiosity. The captain made no effort to receive her but summoned the chief steward.

Suffering from heightened awareness and therefore tense, she was conscious of a swarthy man brooding on the rail. She saw how his elbows rested along the varnished mahogany, and his feet lightly on the teak deck. His ship was a smart one. He wore khaki denims and his head bare (always, until he sailed into his home port). Both of us remember this moment when we exchanged a hard abstract embrace.

He did not move, he did not turn his head, he remained utterly remote and still: thinking, probably, about his wife.

Anna, my wife Anna. The clever, bustling creature who inhabited his flat in Haifa with the child must be some subsidiary character: adored, adoring, satisfactory, equal. To the mother of his child he was kind. But Ilario could not give to any person, infant, body, soul: that which he has, and keeps, for Anna.

The passenger will know her. The past dominates their exhaustive dialogue. She learns the dead Anna, her voice, skin, touch, her hands. The folklore and myth of childhood, the circumstances of disease. The enfolding. It all grew in their imagination. Anna tangible, solid, substantial.

He kisses her: it is Anna, is not Anna, or is his wife freed from inhibition. Between us we create her again. And a disapproving sunbather whisks off snorting when we hold each other's hands. We are innocent, the passenger or that awkward and distant English Anna would have cried. Presently our relationship will overflow from the dining table and the boat-deck into bed. Anna is there, being the purpose of it. The spirit. We may make love and speak of her in the same breath. This and this and this. Here my mouth, here her lips, feeling Anna's fingertips a hundred times more hesitant than yours. She was so small, poverina, whispered Ilario (conscious of the paper-thin bulkhead), and perpetually silent.

Slowly, quietly, gently. The passenger peers at such a brown man, physically perfect, many years older than herself, with whom she is copulating, with great pleasure.

The weather held. Fine blue days followed the ship. Our sea is calm, then choppy. It is windy. Waves curl, white crested. The sun burns. A song-thrush makes landfall upon us, it blows away soundless, helpless. There's a fair breeze, from the starboard quarter, westerly. Huge banks of cloud, cumulonimbus. At night, suddenly, a starless sky. The sea changes its deep colour: grey, green, blue, black. In the chart-room Ilario plotted the great circle route.

I watched. I watched him, a fastidious, conscientious captain. A fusspot, unable to delegate, unpopular with his officers, worshipped by the men. I noticed the slightly rancid atmosphere. I wondered if it had been poisoned through Ilario's inability to trust, to behave. They thought me pretty thick with the old man.

Inadvertently, constantly, she reminds me of Anna. I'm summoned and it's pointed out to me that my precious passenger has climbed the mizzen mast. She was hitched 60ft high. The deck is hard. If she falls I'd be a fool, the Company do not underwrite such ventures.

He smiles. Ilario's dignity does not permit him to go aloft: he leaves the bridge and emerges on deck below her. He signals come down. She grins, or he thinks she is grinning. Her clothes flap, cracking on her back. He cannot hear. She waves: I can't hear. Ilario shrugs, he walks towards the fo'c'sle, Anna in his mind's eye. From the bow he looks into the water. The water moves by at a steady twenty two knots. The water splits, splits, splits. A moment, and she will arrive. You really shouldn't do that, how you are like Anna. Their wrists touch. Their watch straps meet. Their watches tell the time. It is not now. Could you put her out of her misery? the girl asked him.

The salt, the spray, dragged at his lungs.

Curious, perhaps, but the disposal of pain, of persons in pain and intolerable ideas, occurs merely at points in time not relative to a real situation. When one is oneself involved, the thought is carefully, trustingly aborted.

He'd prefer to talk about tankers which disappear leaving no trace. He wanted a tanker, a fully automated beast of burden. A stabilised explosion. A swimming pool. His comforts, creature comforts. He wasn't a tanker man. He was

the father of a child aged two. He was aged forty. And his
wife disliked the sea.

His passenger's fingers rarely fidget. Anna's trembled in
a jitter of energy. This lethargic, peaceful girl: why were they
both so sad. Saddening. You are untypical, an enigma, she
says. She contemplates his flat stomach, the proportions of
his flesh and marrow.

A storm enclosed the vessel in dense shadow off Finisterre.
The damp misty rain set like a seal of misery. We regarded
each other briefly, kindly.

The Israeli agent bounds on board. It is Gideon, the old
friend. Gideon has quickly gathered that they are sad at
parting. Ilario goes ashore for dinner and a game of bridge,
she takes the train to Paris. Gideon says: Anna was a bitch,
she wore the trousers, she surely sailed master of Ilario's ship.

A CAUSE OR OCCASION OF
KEEN DISTRESS OR SORROW
2

or *grief* who manifests himself strangely. I am brilliantly happy, my face split by grins of such rapture, the lips gaping promiscuously. I fly, I float. I walk on air. Some time later I bolt back to sea suddenly.

Gone my relish for the undertaker's jolly lady who handled the photographed coffins like pornography, who slid me breasts—nipples, ginger, brown—and bottoms—thin, fat, oak, chestnut—these genital exposures with alternative furniture. She has a wispy snicker, then two, we shuffle the views, loudly speaking together. Vital perfusion is a procedure during which mammals are embalmed alive costing seven guineas extra: saline solution introduced being a substitute for blood, heart beat beating, organs function-affective, follow o fallacious formaldehyde, to coddle, or suffering as an egg must pickled in icing glass while still fertile. Peek at the weather, she said, you'll soon realise it's hotter: people don't keep. I do solemnly recommend your Anna to be sanitised.

I was by this word brought up with a jolt. Net curtains at the pearly window quiver. Uncompromisingly respectable tis plain she offers not her body own: and I see gorgons, beehive hares writhing, beautiful snakes, worms, all exceeding fat.

Thy bosom hath unto itself a oneness like a unicorn horn, n'er i cleft. She beamed. Teeth in the mouth creep. Dying can't be cheap. Wretched man, he's as white as a sheet. The tock clicks. Here we drain both blood and money, the price frightful. Nonetheless. She was wonderfully human: or ordinary.

Ho ho ho: laughs my registrar of births and death(s). The previous body a. His recent cause (of death) stated. My last chap was. Shh. Lepro see. Surprises never cease. Straight faces are highly important. Most English survivors recoil. Iodine on a ghost. Thus they feel their particular grotesquerie: less. Please do sit down, he remarked. Though that chair may be infected by the poors of a leper's relation, dead skin patches grow regularly. Ilario squatted.

The doctor kindly signing the certificate had an Indian name. You mayn't read it: the envelope is addressed to me. Such insults remain sacred, unintended for secular eyes. Imagine the deceased muddled with another. Dispute disallowed. Circumstances permitting. Objects exist in my office to distract your attention—a ticking clock, the picture frame hung on the empty wall—when I: copy in my legible masculine black handwriting deploying utter integrity intelligence across a necessary job of incredible te deum for this caramel wop husband to a good English gel and accurately absolute innumerable certifications of certificate accepting in payment half the sum involved at a future date.

His window to the world as lofty as his mind. It looks towards the place where the hospital was, the height is the height of Anna's room. Someone medical communicates with someone clerical utilising the dependants, themselves harbingers of, bringers of information, not vital but mortal, not waving but drowning. Now, said the registrar, now. Go to the department of social security, apply for the death grant, we give you six months.

Ilario sensed an alienation in London. He ached, unclean, to contract a banishing disease such as. He was a mental leper, would seem leprous the rest of his: leper's life.

In his hand he held a piece of paper, often repeated. Ovarian carcinoma. Lymphoma. Cerebral haemorrhage (2).

My wife's brother Richard heaped with hothouse flowers the bedside he did decline to visit. Saying, better let her get on with it, nothing I can do by being there. He greeted Ilario. A bracing bonhomie hid his emotional discomfort. I stumble at the threshold of pain and disaster. Richard and Maxwell have had a teeny quarrel, stand staring. A total stranger I. But Maxwell's soft heart is suddenly touched: the traffic, thick tonight? Obviously neither knows. I am bad on the telephone especially in English to this frigid man. The friend flexed his fingers, hugged a batik cushion, gurgled: er, how is she? Richard's ruddy sister. Swallowing, Ilario spoke of her death.

Richard assumes you incompetent to make the arrangements. He drew himself together, why. Authority I have, managed men always, why, why. Because you give an impression of helplessness duckie. Maxwell turned aside unable to bear it. Richard experiences real dramas, life: two mornings ago a scene, Max in the bath drowns downing barbiturates pretending his existence valueless. Snuffed out relations are small fry, you look hungry said her Richard kindly.

Chocolate biscuits crawl across a plate with red roses, eat me exhausted. Gobble him. Stay for a meal, persists he fondling a paunch bulge. Bilge. Stay for ecstasy. I am free, free.

Ilario refused incoherently. They are baffled. You wish to see her. Richard's aghast. We push this sort of thing under the carpet, old chap. Choke on your phlegm. Weeping for men is out. His eyes quite colourless.

Inspired. Ilario ran to his room tore his clothes from their drawers: a hotel, eh eh, shrewd Maxwell silently folds in tissue and delicate affection silk shirts Ilario rarely uses yet possesses, a splendid notion, you are certain, may you feel lonely, hotels impersonal, in touch we'll keep you. Extraordinary, Italians. A blessing to be rid of hysterical him, giggling they debate whether he'll go mad. Acting the parts in a lunatic bin: control, darling, yourself.

Fix tea for the funeral.

Tea.

Naturally. Sandwiches, dark plum cake, strong cups of tea.

I said, very well.

buried According to her Will. It is my wish that I be buried simply and without undue expense and should I die whilst in a foreign country it is my wish to be buried there. Vaguely he wondered about the sea. Did she die whilst the balance of her mind was disturbed? Is that the foreign country? Abroad somewhere she wrote her name.

Interred: says the funeral parlour floosie, we're more posh in the metropolis.

Prosaically to be buried means finding a parson to mutter the words ordained correctly. Poetry not religion. Nice music thumped out on a village organ not sanctification. Sanitisation not sacrilege or (smell). Anna cherishes tradition, by traditional ritual she goes to ground. Tis the quaintest final journey. She shall therefore be dumped, slithered, slotted into a giant muddy vagina. Yea the crude lips of it (mother earth) concealed with imitation grass. Inserted upon soft titillating ropes. The country churchyard of her childhood yields a truly seductive cunt. No other place could have been so idyllic—a shallow singing river beyond a stone wall fashioned for eternity and lolling peaceably across the meadow, cows. Anna lies (rests) close to her father. Both watery graves. Twilight hymns within the church: the radiant husband rolls along the aisle as if at sea (at sea, not knowing where one is). Confounded, she'd have loved to have lain atop him. A fresh breeze catches their clothes, she is better protected, ruffles reach right up to her chin. The coffin he chooses makes a dull perceptible shine. Purple hands, red rural faces, a single posh pallbearer in gloves. Gravelly path, shorn turf like a nun's skull.

Speak these mortal words. Soon we take the sacrament of good cucumber sandwiches, drink the hot tea, an entertainment no one will thank for. The conjuror's eye was complete. I quietly blow my nose. It is still summer.

And he casts morbid gloom over the whole ship—his happiness, his grief, his rapture. Dry land a nightmare, Ilario flew. To Genova, the safety of the sea. She's new to me, I am an unknown quantity to those that sail in her, oh such a clumsy old girl between my legs verminous with fellow men, my own real sunlit world, do I not dream the sweetest dreams inside her creaking aching guts? Sleep ceases, dreams continue: il crepusculo, l'aura: my extremes of temperament and her age alienate the crew, melancholy being an affliction they know nothing about. She is elderly so I love her.

a corpse, Anna, *my* corpse: I demand to view the remains. Come captain dearie a ward sister accompanies thee on a trip (we walk miles from the healing part: suddenly the hospital seems very gothick). I do hopefully anticipate clean pragmatic marble slabs for purposes of cooling my mind. You are doomed to disappointment: the little woman struggles at a huge door, ornately oaken, marked mortuary, and oiled not to squeak. The bereaved has forgotten his gallantry: I offer my fist and touch her hair, embarrassing us. She says wait, popping through a crack, allow me to ascertain whether our exhibit's properly prepared. I place my nose eyes ears one inch from the oak. You may proceed: we enter. Astounded, he cannot believe the sight which meets them. A beloved wife awaiting my respects I see stretched (racked) at a height of where is my mouth. A plinth, an altar. Abnormally long, she occupies much space. They have festooned me in chrome-coloured embroidery, bilious body yellow. Kneel. No. A christian cross weighs upon my chest. Prayer is the last thing I contemplate. It's not permitted. A prie-dieu provided free. A pectoral anchor, nay a great petrified stone to sink me. My cotton wool tickles: she wants, I think, to sneeze, Sister. I want to laugh unimaginably. Golden drapes, dangling like gilded penises, obscure a wall without windows: suitable, suitable, monstrous vulgarity. And how delightful this damask, this death, this odourless cave, delicious: he murmurs at the treat. She notices the homesick Italian smiling as if smiling at his wife. She shuffles her feet shyly, it is her duty. Farewell to Anna leaving.

THE CARRYING OF A PERSON TO ANOTHER PLACE OR SPHERE OF EXISTENCE

3

a definition of rapture, relative and definitive, or infinite, not finite, but final; people in moments of great emotion, places of the body in physical excitation, the flesh in parts of rapture, by another person or the same person made; spheres of departure, beyond a limit, reaching this limit, defining it, empirically; and then, knowing it; in a moment ending, or the moment ending.

Anna, the wife that I have, strains, my cock like a corkscrew, she arches her back, pleading. There is something I want, Ilario must give me, I must give him, must give us, must give myself, must give. It is me, in me, between us, not him, his: fault. Let it be now. It is not.

And la fica weeps without ceasing, endlessly, of my own dearest, there's no limit to these tears from the womb, the moment never comes, oh she is so bitter to taste, sour in my mouth, on my tongue. Or, vinegar to wash the anguish, and in my hands a sponge of perpetual sorrow.

Acid of our marriage, strange, symbolic, a mortification. The wormwood, shadow, deadly belladonna, gall. Her cunt streaming: caressing ourselves we are stung: kissing, I poison him. Better the stiff coquettish bride than an aching female, a cow which I a bull serve. Thus two of us celebrate male fertility, mine. Making but a fatal repetition, heart-rending, our love, the failure, a recognition: here, suckling my penis, clasping and unclasping, innocent and virginal, myself within her; here the true and final incompleteness, inadequacy, inhumanity. Unjust.

Starkly, Ilario said: Anna, is that all you feel? Puffed up and swollen, red; a child's eyes crying. He said: you must pretend. Pretend? Pretend? He was stunned, scornfully, poked her legs apart, the shame. But how? I cannot imagine what I do not know.

Beginning: an orgy of remorse. Thin though Anna is, I am copulating with a whale. I ride, together we heave in hope, her breasts little squabs, skin and gristle, flippers, deformities, porpoise fins, I touch blubber, our legs arms bellies beat frantically. I sense blood throbbing against my caked nails. Murdering her, peculiar, tail, until she screams for relief, tugs at my fingers: it's no use, you are only hurting me. Hating her, loving her.

She blames her ugliness, you are not ugly, or her child-hood, me, him, I shall die unknowing, you deny me, no *no*, I regard the brain, despair. Everything a human body can in tenderness do, I do. You don't understand: why am I angry. But we are both humiliated. We are married. Let us approach the problem rationally. I am taking you to a doctor. I won't go, I won't. Adamant. Anna fights, refuses, hysterical. I am someone who never pretends, she said sadly. It obviously isn't enough. She lies listening to her husband—this and this and this, is what other women do. Perhaps Englishmen don't mind.

I sail without her. Bewildered, she fancies me fornicating wildly in foreign ports. She is wrong; I am faithful. Consumed by a new compassion so intense I confound myself. Separately we sleep, week after week, month after month, the days pass, passed. Disarranged, distorted, we try again. Or we are exhausted.

She waits for me one summer in Naples. Often taking the hydrofoil to Capri and to Ischia. Favourite islands, favourite beaches, as constricted as she is, and as crowded. She swims, hot from the bus. Utterly alone, lonely, wading into the clear green water, red sunburnt skin, the embrace, yes, of warm sea. Anna the person swimming.

She shuddered, prolonged, convulsive, almost drowning in ecstasy: is that, this, then, it? she asks Ilario pathetically, could the moment in Forio d'Ischia, be it. Solemnly he shook his head: nel mare? very well, we shall invoke the help of the sea. He seemed happy, she was crestfallen.

They go at sunset, he and his elderly wife, into an island harbour, where it's quiet, where no one else is about, and he undresses her a long way out. Their feet fumbling on the sand below briefly. Pressing hard, giggling, clammy. The feel rather lacking. She swallows, wants to swim away, shocked. In his toes wrinkled ground, in his hands the crack of her crutch: he grips, they shift. He stuffs his cock up her, piece by piece, more fingers than genuine propulsion, feeding a goose forcibly. It is funny, she said. It's bit grotesque. The salt was astringent. She felt a cold insulation between skins. Even the uncircumcised penis rasped back and forth. At least it was original: and she kept an eye on the beach. He is dying to come, her staunch disapproval entertains, quickly, quickly, the boiling semen, soon it has all run into the sea. Ilario laughed too much to be disappointed.

There is a pain, swelling, gestating in the guts, indistinct, dull, for which one must compromise. Her dreaming grows explicit, she goes so far and no further, the spinster espoused, he puts his arm—in the dream—around her waist, she is enthralled simply by the sensation of comfort, he takes her hand, and she trembles. You have a lovely touch he tells his creature kindly and she's appalled, the anomaly possesses her, she struggles.

To have and to hold, from the deepest grief springs the greatest pleasure, our dear sister, do deliver her out of the miseries of this sinful world, created me in an image, by mutation, the glass shatters, unable to record my weather, furniture removals, thunder, castrated lightning: you are babbling, Anna, your words make no meanings.

You will scatter and sow, some seeds shall cause an obsession, malignant, unbenign, to flourish, darken, and she longed to practise the novelty, carnal knowledge, to obliterate twenty desolate years, her adulthood. Ilario is amazed at the intensity, energy, absolutism, the diabolical drive of her: undoubtedly, passion, was possible.

Not characters in a drama: ciphers. Evil and good.

Because he spends time at a distance remote from home, Anna, at the mercy of imagination, wakes worn out and sopping, frozen. Maybe I can exist merely in the imagination, she says: he thinks her raving. You don't realise, totally, Ilario, how I feel diminished. He wonders, is it such an importance? admitting that it is. Reflected in her whole personality, aggression, shyness, dominating certainly, the outward compensation for inward deficiency, inner distress. Why must I be hideous? she whispers, naked. For ever cursed with my own flesh blood bones, tears. Tears? I may cry, said Ilario, your eyes remain hauntingly dry. Arid.

And in my ship she grows hopeless, helplessly conscious of the dividing bulkhead, a fragile membrane of her mind to which a suffering deck officer next door lends an alert omnipresent ear. We lie coupled stifling our voices, while what is lost steadily drips between our legs onto the bed. Hearing the knob turned on his radio she's anguished, reluctantly I sympathise, less squeamish, more generous than Anna permits. Sleep now for dreaming, loving done elsewhere. We shall never love each other, said this: wife. Losing hope. Losing much. She was unable to perceive my rapture.

Easter came early, oddly chill at the coast. Fog, dampening and corroding of spirits. Ilario and Anna began a journey, inland, to the sun. A mystical journey. Nightingales still sing in Italian woods. There was snow on the mountains, ferocious heat beneath. They bought panini, wine, olives, cheese, chocolate Baci wrapped in a silver riddle. And lay, unadventurously, two together, silent, to the sound of felling trees, chopping noises, country echoes. In a copse. In a valley. Somewhere in Italy. Ilario gently twists her hair. Watching him munching, drinking, licking lips, wiping his mouth, blowing his nose. Having eaten he smiles and drops into a doze. His eyelashes fluttering.

Anna examined him, aware and alive. He sighed. Seeing his ears, neat as a child's, and his neck, faint with down. My ugliness, your comeliness—my love. She says it aloud. His warmth vanishes into thin air, it's all wasted. She bent over him. She wished: touch me—kiss my agonies, wounds, pains, blemish. She supposes he has at this moment—she pretends. She does pretend. She does.

TIME THAT IS TO BE
OR COME HEREAFTER

2

Ilario returns to the cottage. A close relation has come to collect her clothes. The damp has got into them, she says accusingly. He made coffee. Together, silent friends, they look at Anna's chest of drawers, wardrobe, and shoe cupboard. It is winter, outside the rain is falling, wildly he strips Anna's sister quite naked in his mind. But she's a bright young woman of forty, not at all the same. She smokes hard, showering ash. Lipstick on the filter. Her legs are clean and white. The skirt above sheer tights stretches over a rubbery bum. Anna wore, like animal hide, corsets. Until this moment among the suitcases Ilario has not completely realised the difference. His wife's stale garments are those of an old woman. Huge silky bloomers, woolly vests or bodices, dozens of darned stockings. Shapeless inexplicit trousers made from strange unfashionable material. Viyella blouses, almost new. Hats, gloves, horny handbags, for three decades of weddings, christenings, funerals. Dresses bought to fit a bigger person, slack even on hangers. Shoes, without smell. Enormous curling brogues, molded by bunions, corns, crooked toes. With tiny pockets of mud stuck bone dry to the soles. Squashed because she walked badly. Stained slippers worn furless. Many many jerseys, mainly mauve, lavender, violet, purple. Tweedy coats. A lot of ancient macks, her beloved Burberrys. Sewing things, buttons in tins, picture hooks, safety pins. Hankies in scented sachets. Hairbrushes. The dressing table seems worst. Anna was mucky, she spilt. Dark pink powder puffs up in sudden nauseating clouds. Also she possessed seven empty pots of Ponds Cold Cream, and lips everlastingly sore, raw, lately bitten. Then jewellery, lumpy stones such as amber, garnet. Pomegranate. Ivory beads, her mother's engagement ring, some valuable broken bits in a box. Ilario is dismayed, wishing it gone, magicked away. A whole jumble sale crosses the floor. Slowly his sister-in-law turns, touches, folds, piles. Curious. Don't you want to keep this? she asks. I prefer memories. Mmm? *We think her husband mad.* Ilario, she repeated, pronouncing his name at arm's length, distastefully mouthing it, Il-ah-rio. Poking in a fresh cigarette. Pity, I have no matches. My lighter's bust. He supplies a small flame. Blunders, bumps her, mumbles sorry. Leaving her to it he wandered off. The place mine. In which I spent only a few days each year, Anna was alone or it was shut up, the stuff is hers in it, not mine, I own two sextants, our worldly goods are my wife's, the past belongs to Anna, she hoarded, she cherished, therefore I share the past with the past, her family, otherwise I shall be unfree, objects can be remembered easily. Upstairs, boards creak. He finds a piece of line and ties a turk's head on the kitchen broom. Clever, how clever! she exclaimed. Ilario smiled. The favourite relation could cuddle the poor man: she doesn't dare. China, glass. You may take. Really, really. Your home breaks. But on board it already has been provided, I don't need a habitation here, a glass remains a glass, we might smash her rosy china cup, her early morning tea. Horrified by his latin emotion she casts her eyes to the ceiling as he dashes the crockery to the floor saying: highly satisfactory, symbolism. Oh, she replied doubtfully, feeling trapped. Ilario packs a few treasures, her books, a photograph album. I don't see we can transport so much. Another journey, have a key, she is very pleased, where are you sleeping, tonight Southampton I hope, and the house? Decisive, he has instructed an agent, not bothered: peculiar, thought his wife's sister. They lug cases to her car, it fills to the brim, Anna's car too will be loaded. Lunch? she inquired, I'm peckish. The electricity's cut at the main, switch it on, no, they go to the pub, strolling jerkily along the road. She is taller than he is, he glances towards her nose, a prettier nose, Anna's was very definite. In the pub he recognises hardly a soul. The lunch disgusts him. Yesterday he passed the churchyard forgetting the funeral once celebrated there: his recovery after recent bereavement. The grave has healed, has grown grass, it calls for a headstone. Gone indecency, come clothing. She sips her beer, searching her handbag for cigarettes. More beer. Ilario speaks from the heart as if to the woman beside him: nevertheless I begin a time of unimaginable loneliness which is not remotely to do with being lonely or alone, tis an excluded state, putting my previous self in some inaccessible place irretrievable at will, and I'm cut like a root in the ground, my greenery extinguished, deprived. A numbness, no, nor a deathwish, nor uncontrollable grief: instead a sensation so bleak, empty, devoid of character. She smoothed her hair. She isn't grey. And her eyes are opaque, the irises clearly unringed. Not sure about reality. He nudges her thigh. By mistake, firm, hot. Apologies. A nod and she frowns. He plotted a course, the ship's gyro held it and by simplest dead reckoning one arrived in another place, or position. Places identical. Roughly the same daily speeds. Slowed with a stiff wind at the head, chased in a following gale. Weather changes, waves, swell, directions, forces, cloud heights, amounts covering the sky. He rose to buy their third drinks, the bar held a sophisticated olive, he ate it. He gave orders, the orders executed he wondered why? In port the usual problems prevail, are solved, are not solved, we put to sea, with them, without them. We raise derricks, we lower derricks, then we sit on them and paint them orange, white, grinning faces meet me. Open hatches, secure hatches. Load, off-load, the cargo manifest lies on my desk. And I'm perfectly happy, content. Excuse me, said Ilario, I must have been lost in thought. Confused. She acknowledged this, a trifle ironically. Dabbing her, nose, the handkerchief monogrammed, initial A, she has borrowed Anna's, he stares through the window. People, especially people, seem separated, separate from me, seem objects, just inanimate objects, and I'm the outsider, the outcast, their world, their idiom, is not mine. Their world, an ant-heap, looks fun: mine could be, and isn't, any longer, fun. My sense of humour vanishes, I have none. His bored companion scratches her knee: nails, Anna's translucent nails? red varnish obscures. She scratches heartily, using the balls of her fingers, Anna scratched with nails, hypersensitive and intense. Absolutely nothing funny happens, I think humourlessly, in no mood to smile. It is grim, it is black, I care about not a person on earth, equally am not cared about. There may be an after, there was a before: the now is intolerable. The base of his glass stood in a little patch of wet. I drink alcohol often, I smoke infrequently hash, it doesn't matter, it doesn't alter me. I know silence surrounds me. Silence. Then, at that moment, a different awareness, a science fiction overtakes the tortoise: my personality is: changing. Changes. I trust: I haven't strained a muscle. She says rubbing a leg. I hope you haven't, I like you: warmly. She is most beautiful mute. He spent whole days staring into space. In secret we suspect Ilario to be glad, we resent his youth, Anna should die an old maid, inviolate(d), she might survive twenty true years, *we are fond of Anna too*, he was merely the husband, unsuitable husband, what possessed her I imagine? The sister saw his olive skin, she squirmed. Ilario's eye caught her breast, the bulge beside a shorn armpit, nice roundness. He wanted to touch it with the back of his hand obliquely. Had god given double femininity to a plump rosy body, could he find Anna's missing parts scattered between these legs, in these mouths, lips, eyes, across acres of unscarred flesh? He smelt, distending his delicate nostrils, smelt their beer. Oh Anna drank children's drinks—pineapple, coca cola, fizzy pop—through a plastic straw. Shall us have one, more, to keep our, strength, going. He agrees, shall I, and you, return, in full strength to the stripped mattress of our bed, lie on it pretending like children or chiavare, screw? Now let me lay my dear departed's sister. Open her coffin lid. I will perform upon the corpse tormented in an eternal orgasm. You vicariously might surrender identity for a five minute (funeral) service, I ejaculate into that monogrammed handkerchief, adorn our burial mound in daffodil seed, may we make everlasting flowers in your sister's fica? She asks at the bar for their table to be wiped, carries frothy mugs spilling nothing. Yes, my personality changes. I act spontaneously: these actions are not mine. I discover my self, it dawns on me that my self has died, her self is rooted in my body and mind. Which is a nonsense I reject utterly. What is dead was dead has died. Anna definitely died. We plonked her mortal remains in the good earth of Wessex, blessed the skeleton in time to come. I swear so. But. Modern and mundane, I

telephone and tear strips off people. Not I. Articulate, per-
suasive, in a foreign language, I argue. Ilario never argued.
A voice was unnecessary. Anna needed a voice, she depended
on words to attract fellow humanity, failing, and I did not,
surely do not, yet astonished acquaintances, baffled, recoil.
She existed atop a sulphurous volcano: it spewed her out and
sucked her in. Such spiritual intensity was unusual. Cigarette
smoke billowed round the man's face, he coughed. It embraced, gathered him together, he wanted to kiss her. Sorry,
so sorry, she says, waving the thick blue air. I do think, speak,
feel, as Anna: more as I know Anna did. I search for excuses,
coincidences, I dismiss it as grief, weariness, or lunacy. Bitterly I resent the spooky battle within. The absurdity: I don't
believe. And later I learn to enjoy being: possessed. Shall we
depart? She stumbles, he helps her to stand, she crushes the
last fierce cigarette. Have you been dreaming. It's days since
we saw the sun. She blinks. I release her. She is a stranger.
Mmm, she remarked, mmm. She grinned, frigid, alien, far
from rape. Hostile. They stagger to the house and clothes.
Possessed. Imagination makes mistakes. Much as I love Anna
I treasure Ilario. Quite easily the explanation rests in a ris-
orgimento, my identity stifled at marriage, abruptly exposed.
Pale, nude the worms beneath a stone, admitted to reality
after an absence in hades. He shivered. Cold? No not really.
Fortunate to be a person who rarely feels cold. One notices—
she talks, polite, making loud noises with her feet—that
people born in hot countries aren't much troubled by our
wretched climate.

THE STATE OF TIME
OF BEING A CHILD

2

Whiskery, he kissed, fondled, tickled, groped, sat us upon his knees. Then, duty done, he disappeared.

My father.

My father was portly. He had a large frame. Fair hair, prematurely silver, and small blue eyes. Men's eyes twinkled as a matter of course. In those days. The old days. Our darkness came from Mum. Her colouring dominated his, obliterated it, making his own family look as though we weren't. Temperamentally, I am said by one and all to be exceedingly alike him. Not an easy man to know.

I was eleven when.

When I was eleven he: set out for a walk, to the other side of the woods, at two precisely in the afternoon. And in this wood of ours wild anemones still grow. He passed brimble bushes, primroses, beneath sweet chestnuts he prodded the soft peat with his cane. Or was it a stout walking stick. He strode through gorse, bracken, heather. Ling heather. At a time, simply *at a time*, the moment never to be established, he arrived. The river was at full spring flood: that we know full well. Full, everything: replete, satiated.

Tying his spaniel strangled to a tree, into the river he: stepped. Or fell.

Badly bitten.

I picture Dad dragging an elephantine leg towards the edge. Oh, hot blood rushing, pounding, surrounding his head. Power to the brains. Agony. Beautiful water. I adore water. It.

Where the bank drops sheer and shiny and the mud is polished, I squat, watching reflections. His face, my face. In the stagnant silence died a man, spoiling the fishing. Lo, the coarse pike twists. I sit eating bitter chocolate. Pointing—here the spot, he sank accidentally while his balance was disturbed. Yonder that mound marks his spaniel's early grave. These my secret expeditions to attend a suicide.

Domestic animals share our fate. The dog could have strangled spontaneously at the awesome sight. Dear master drowning. Dead dogs don't talk, observed Dad's gamekeeper, a morbid wit. Dad carried no gun.

Events had little order. It was left to us to imagine the drama.

Perhaps the adder, alarmed, swimming in the fast current, bit a man already drowned.

No.

Because he was previously swollen. One leg exceeded by five times the size of its mate. Also, he was all puce.

Sakes alive.

The snake hurt, striking through the many clothes he wore for the time of his death. Poison dispersed rapidly. A vein in the thigh ruptured. His tie loosened. His tie was never found.

Perfect, accurate, odd.

Demented, did he seek relief. *Do not run, proceed at a steady pace to the nearest human habitation.*

A stickler for elementary first aid.

So he rested, dickey the heart, supine or prone: had he stood the adder would have been restricted to the shin. True, the wild wood writhed with adders in high summer: we whistled to warn them, and obediently, modestly, they'd slide away. What had Dad done to annoy a viper.

Every tree, every bush, we strip each tree and bush naked: but nothing can be determined.

A mile below the weir, laid out on a rotten jetty, the body isn't him.

I say Dad got damnably fed up, murdered a gipsy. This accounts for the snake bite, which provided a disfiguring disguise. Quite clever. But in the past he has been most particular and nice about gipsies, letting them gather faggots, holly, and nuts. A town person, therefore, a no good picking daffodils to sell in the square. Well, whoever we bury it won't decompose any relation.

I prepare to meet my father lurking in the rhododendrons, hoping for a glimpse of his children. Anna shall shield you from your horrid wife. Bring crab sandwiches to the shrubbery. And so on. In years to come, when I've grown up and gone, my faithful father, emaciated and depressed, brought at last to his knees, will appear: as if resurrected.

He certainly smelt dead.

Nannie, scandalised, said: Anna you shouldn't have been to see it dear. It's enough to give us *nightmares*.

So it did, and for all my life.

Ah disbelief. Or: I wonder what drowning can do to the memory.

Once I fell face downwards in the sea, an innocent toddler. Mum ran, abandoning her skirt, she tweaked me from the waves, performing her only maternal act since my birth. I recall a swirling sensation. I am grateful.

They drag the river. Does he, drowning, think of me? The weed drifts across my face. May a vision come. My head reaches the surface. My hair soaks floating in a slow flowing river. I must know how it feels. My mind is washed away in this cold murky water.

And at night, in the dark, I'm alive in the coffin breaking bones with him. Trying to raise the lid. The oak screeches, gleaming, seasoned. The screws are golden, they are brass.

His knees made raw, his fists red blubber, he measures a miserable mortal strength against the solid earth above him where some flowers droop. Blood seeps from our eyes. The callous sexton is stone deaf. If simple narcissi can hear, lend us an ear, we pray. Lighten our darkness.

Or in that twilight it was right and meet to hold hands. His pale pudgy hands rips the shroud, he farts like a sow, we whisper politely together, in an extremely confined space. Saying, surely it's *wrong* to bury people living still.

Gone to heaven. In my dreams I visit heaven and I wet my bed. Nannie: thoroughly over-excited if you ask me. The funeral service wasn't too terribly nice.

Or I tiptoed, forbidden, to *their part of the house.* His bedroom, his dressing room. Stinking of badgers, of tobacco, or his maleness. His name was sewn ostentatiously everywhere: it crawled over the pillow, across each silk shirt and onto all the lawn handkerchiefs. These were his possessions. I snuffled amongst his clothes. Then the strange slumberer moved, and I fled.

The air in her room heaved not with scent but cloying violence: daily she threw cut glass jars at maids, split her silver brushes banging on the wall. Hating her own face, though she was very handsome, perpetually she peered into the mirror: if looks could kill she shattered it. Oh god.

We wore grey for the funeral. No jet black horses trot to the door: a common motor hearse paused in the drive. No ostrich plumes. No tears. But an unfortunate bumble bee died, distraught, ensnared by her veil. I wonder how bad human flesh tastes: but neither were we forced to eat at the feast.

I forage the grave. My unresponsive distant father—vaguely important as a purveyor of cash, the butcher who filleted his wife's inherited riches—is transformed, vanishing to reappear as a talking, loving, hugging person. As unreal as possible.

My imaginings blossom, become more sophisticated, swell in mind and memory. Now his clothes have fallen to dust, he's nude, and I've cuddled him thus. The moustache lasts, the lashes linger on the sunken eyes.

I long for bedtime, to be by his side.

Our father which art in heaven. Mum says: prayers are heretical, we shall remain heathen, god bless this house and all who suffer in it. Is loving someone evil?

In my character exist my father's worst faults. I resent the comparison, I am unhappy: he took his life away. Aged fifty he died: aged fifty I'll die. My sister crosses her fingers, saying: don't tempt fate. Do stop making remarks about Dad. You bring it upon yourself, my mother mutters, because you're *stupid, awfully stupid*.

Yes, I am alike my father. He was a weak man it is fully accepted. He milked Mum's money. So she begged continuously for more from where that came from: Grandfather, worth over a million when he died. To him Dad seemed utter dead wood. Modernisation had been needed in the mill and capital sums intended for the house flowed into other mouths, the gaping greedy gobs of trade, vulgar, unscrupulous. Mum did wild things extravagantly. Horses went lame. The farm lost cream and butter down the drain to the village. Tuberculin testing decimated the Jersey herd. Mum would have been blissful managing a smaller household. It was he who wanted desperately to be grand. He didn't play, quite, cricket. Dad was not an honourable man.

The day my father wandered snake bitten and feverish after murdering a faithful innocent hound through the woods and into the river, he was bankrupt.

It is a ludicrous shock. Concealed from us, his children. A father in financial difficulties. Less, less thrilling. The coffin held no warm cuddler, then, merely dust. My childhood fantasy comes to an end. Suddenly, a watery death, thine or mine, is *horrible*. Did you swallow much? Much water? The pain spread across your chest, creeping like the conceited monograms. Your lungs burst. I see it all before me, love: ah, death is particular, and no death can be particularly nice. Dandelions wither in my bed, over my head. My mouth opens, black torrents pour through my purple lips. Drowning does this to the memory.

He existed, perished, in between he begat me. He was a happening. Which is to say: he occurred, presently obsessed an isolated imaginative child. I claim naught for determinism. I am I myself.

The snake swam to the farther shore.
To know it is impossible.

A CHANGE
BROUGHT ABOUT BY THE SEA

2

She scratches. I watch. She scratches, I listen. Biting my tongue, clenching my teeth. Grit like gravel in the mouth. Forcing myself not to speak to her. She can't help it. For how long, for ever, for more than one whole voyage we shed parts of Anna's menopause around the world, and then, and then, it took at least a year, our torment. It's the scratching I can't forget.

Upon the shin her hand travelled, down each wodge of crepe bandage, over the thick brown stockings. Seeking small sensations, contact with what lay beneath. A highly distinctive sound, human nail on pure lisle, an acquired experience. As she scratches, abstracted, her unconscious pox, staring gloomy and depressed into nowhere, does she suppose I don't care? Shall I say it: you're scratching, again. Will she answer: I'm sorry, angrily. My ears must be abnormal. And she was not: scratching. She merely felt. Feeling makes a strange noise, amore. We glare. I am guilty. Absurd. Yes. But she's unaware of how much she: causes me.

He pounces, she flinches. Does she gnaw her fingers? smoke? twitch? Of course not. The itch becomes unbearable. If she brushes lightly, nails being best, she eases the pain. Must Ilario grudge her that?

Hours they sit, play chess, talk, read. She reads. A hand holds the book, another spidery hand wanders on her leg, creepy, creeping. The books are abandoned, their spines twisted: Anna has extracted these books' guts. In bed, her shoulder dips, she is groping, she is bare—no bandages to allow the air—so, asleep, she scratches. I wake, it continues, oh you are harming your poor places. Still sleeping she stops. Yet I rise, put my wife out of earshot, join two men in the quiet dark wheelhouse. Her legs arrive raw next morning. I bring us coffee from the saloon galley, toast and scrambled eggs. We are companionable. We both look, while she dresses.

A ticklish business, the ship is rolling. I'm terribly tender. I can see you are. Please, don't goggle at me, says Anna. Was I really, goggling? She sighs, he apologises.

We inspect her damage. Below the knees, she's black and blue. Veins bulge obscenely through skin so taut, so tired, it often bursts: special plasters hold the bloodstream back, bleeding unpermitted. Filled with bad blood, cheap petrol, she throbs: this is not the irritation. I ache abominably, she remarks, a bit helpless. Varicose veins our household word. But. Always she has suppurating patches, pus and maggots gather ye rapidly, erupt and infect. Particularly serious about the ankles swollen straight as logs. She prods: I'm puffier. The bone shows white, skin is white, feet are yellow, also there are pretty big green bruises. I find such human landscape a nightmare. And where dying flesh peels, hanging, glued messily to cotton lint; where islands of dead horn cling, shining, heroic limpets; she *hurts*. I want to bend, kiss, cure, heal, this and our minds. But I sit, vast distances between us. Ointment, or is it tar. Fit enough to remedy a better amputation. Too late, prognosis before diagnosis. Bandaged, she walks. In a rough sea, she retreats to a flat bunk, all edges hazardous, our good vessel imperils us: and loving, fucking, four limbs avoid the tiniest bump, trunk into trunk, my cock her cunt, these are our ends, joined, define our limit; it isn't a simple matter. I smile, hoping to encourage her: together with the change of life she catches dermatitis on the legs.

Beginning: new confusion. A woman whose menstrual cycle was farcical—she saved a piddling infertility to stink and seep from the womb only at awkward moments—now floods me in tears, blood, soaks my bed with urine. Bladder, cheeks, tummy, her crimson embarrassments.

Anna, it's no crime: she hides, staggers to the lavatory, a child again, reduced. He laughs. Amused? treating her: nicely. She grips the crutch: my waters break, swimming I shall drown, drained I am lost: hot flush consume me in hellfire.

Railway carriages have no corridors. Taxis pause mindless minutes in traffic jams. The opera they go to never finishes. Napoli a city senza gabinetti: she would welcome a primitive hole in the pavement, and streets to swallow her. She shared one once with an astonished gallant man who peed while she squatted. Or behind the car door, taken short on the autostrada, exasperated but desperate, she did it. The violence appalled us. You are out of the ordinary. I am the same as other females. And she forfeited: control. Emotionally over-whelmed.

You sleep, adulterate, there's someone else, my legs have put you off: I'm jealous, not jealous, you are jealous: will you tell me—what is she like: I hate her. Non-existent. She should exist. I want you happy, Ilario. Let's get you a sensible girl, a glamorous thing. Then she hates all women.

She breaks into weeping, awful because she knows it's cowards who cry. I am powerless to deny these peculiar principles learnt by iron hearts in childhood. She conceals: face, mouth, eyes; and the foul drops in la fica. Thinking she has evil, is unclean. Not interested in logic, remotely.

And doesn't every living soul on board bear witness to her depression, isn't she wrong to be depressed, our bounden purpose in this world being to present cheerful unflagging grins at it? Anna scowls.

Mercifully, she likes the Italian doctor I make her visit. He speaks minimal English so they have a perfect, useless conversation and he pronounces: it will pass. She's satisfied. Surely they accomplished little?

At home a consultant dermatologist talked a lot about the veins, her other worry is commonplace. My wife must suffer, women do. Then she spent a far east trip ashore, alone and, probably, moping. If only they had noticed her dermatitis was cancer of the skin. Alone when it was winter, bitterly cold, extremely and extravagantly wet.

She huddles near the fire, smelling applewood in flames: weird configurations enter me, the shape of flames, an ancient alchemy: scatter I the pavements in our town with purple, ill fortune to they that thereupon do tread: and the power of procreation, leave me. I never needed children, why must it haunt me in my most middle age. Ah, to appear not in command of thyself, Anna. Leaking sensibilities fragile as an infant. A retribution, a solemn curse. A barren wasted life. A bird whistles, she screams, beyond tears, the kettle overboils: this is all too much, far too enormous.

In her imaginings she confounds us by conceiving. He: bleeds to death, decomposes inside my inside. I'm his coffin, his grave, his own words spoken, his blessings. I am the worms, I digest him, eat drink in remembrance of our son. At the rough stone hearth I kneel, peeling stories from my lips, milk from my breast, pretending. The babe melts, anointed in paraffin, promptly I. Husbands return out of the deep sea, as a punishment some severe my tongue is severed at its root, the stub smeared, a lit cigarette, over bright my feverish cheeks. Beet coloured, womb addled, thus the brain. Her period announces Ilario, five months gone: he insists he stirs her with his spoon she implores it is she's sure a mortal sin, grievous clambering onto false gods. I'm disgusting, aren't my legs unpleasant. He says dispassionately, keep them bandaged, keep your stockings on. Copious cries: Ilario's admitted she is less than wholesome. But we're accustomed now to anything.

The firestone explodes, the chips fly in many directions, scalding the carpet. Anna: for a moment, frightened: jumps, startled. Presently she resumed her staring across the small horizon of our sitting room.

Not precognition, prevision. I observe, unknowingly, an image in miniature of her future illness: that staring, especially at objects which stare back—televisions—and reflect a different reality: the self touching, feeling a diseased body, coping with symbolic malign—changing her leaves frequently, a model Eve: and the rehearsal done, she would be better to be worse.

Anna, you bite your lips. My lips are sore. May this seem a reason. A reason. A reason for pimples on my chin, warts in the palm, moles shooting like cultivated mushrooms manured from my armpits. Provide reasonable explanation, because age doesn't come into it. Hair whitens, skin wrinkles, features alter and sag. Indeed I surrender to quixotic emotion at a time of flux, suffer strange maladies, crimson garments, and smell. I am taught eventually to walk slower, I'll hobble with a stick, yes happy. Joints stiffen, bones creak, toes can no longer pick matches barefoot off the deck. This surely is age. Shall I be: desirable. Or will you desire me? Speculations agreeable, peaceable. Temporary problems: dissolve two in water and down sorrow. That part remains: curable. But my evil still is mysterious, is beginning, is an end: I am falling in the crossfire. She cannot sleep.

Transparent, dreamless months. We sail: I was determined to take her. And my wife drifts masculine in stripy pyjamas around us, loving the sea at night, warm nights at sea, rare phosphorous, black familiar oceans. Your gaunt ghost will disturb the sailors. Don't be ridiculous. Wisely I confine her amidships, where she leans on the rail brooding. Yawning. She has an odd characteristic shark snap, I hear those yawns for ever, the metal in her teeth. She rubs on the rail. No one approaches. Anna inviolate. Adamant, refusing barbiturates. The affliction visits feebly, dries up finally. Am I over it? Until he holds her face, traces lines, circles, his hands soothing her neck. Coraggio, said Ilario.

Courage.

A CAUSE OR OCCASION OF
KEEN DISTRESS OR SORROW

3

I am not afraid.

You are riddled with it.

I shall undergo a series of tests, like a nuclear weapon. The hospital does not frighten me, it is my only salvation. Herds of us poor sheep wait drinking sweet tea, or some medical sacrament. Cancer will separate the sheep from the goats, the males from the females.

I recline in a compound glare, fellow men scuttle behind a black screen, invisible rays scan my stomach. The lie detector hums and clicks. I am innocent, innocent. My palms sweat unhealthily. Face downwards I'm in agony. I see the reflection in the shiny machine of the technician's turban. You are uncomfortable, Anna. Ah yes. They help the infirmity to stand.

The doctor has second sight, being a specialist: announcing: she contracted contagious hepatitis in Hong Kong (harbour). Ilario coddled me according to the *Sea Captain's Practical Medical and Surgical Manual*, pages 96–99, which has the coloured appearance of a good cookery book: measles and spotted dick, syphilis and syrup, stuffed marrows, burst appendices, a cheese soufflé curried with rice: we studied your blood, and given the state of your liver, we assume it was not ordinary jaundice even if the captain did keep rat guards on all lines ashore. Your swollen, highly sensitive liver is permanently damaged, dear.

In the path lab they prised reluctant droplets from her fingerprints, grilled them, and thus gleaned information out of the past. Anna's wedding ring clanked on their formica table. She spun it nervously, shrinking visibly like poor Augustus. Take one triangular razor blade, several microscope slides, a wad of cotton wool, draw the eyes dagger, and *stab*. A whole day doing little pricks: how depressing.

Or: from a pectoral cavity jealously hoarding its visceral secrets, a student filled a quart can enticing unspeakable liquid along size 10 knitting needles driven through the ribs. Then Anna wished heartily to be cast naked on a desert island or in a desert to wither blistered by the sun. She felt thrown to the wolves. She felt that vultures would have done the job on her better. She felt sure she was a giant turtle slowly slain ten miles from Mururoa atoll. The pale youth patted her bare back saying splendid, smiling. Try guessing the number of knobbles on your spine. She grinned, or did she really grimace.

Chemicals shall clear your chest of further annoyances. Caustic, to cauterise the heart. Chemistry causes the hair to leave my scalp, she murmured, as a totally bald eagle passed in a wheelchair? True, you and he both have similar vaguely internal problems. But we prescribe different potions, never fear. Men can take their punishment: women, ah, women are too soft and sensitive to it. So she braced her brain, flexed her feet, asked: do I by any chance have *cancer*. And the chap in charge of her case answered (speaking strictly): no. His little philosophical quibble seemed ethically correct.

Not content with the blood, the piss, and the unspeakable

liquid, they sliced her skin, delved between her old bones. Thus retrieving a lymph gland, for analysis. Also: a bronchoscopy was performed. There could be no end to the trouble and the time, the giving and the taking. An inexhaustible energy, directed towards Anna's individual survival.

For this is the silent defiant world: she looks through the window and in the streets like throats which surround or radiate her wondercure-palace sees men and women wandering with their faces mapped, a tragedy in blue indelible ink.

The outpatient sought refuge from her brother Richard and his oily Maxwell in a London park which no longer seemed a travesty of the countryside she cherished. But didn't the trees have dutch elm disease? lie felled? smoulder, fires lit in their guts? Then she became too bad to go unless driven, then too bad to go, then too bad. She stayed at Richard's cosy flat quite often during the two years her illness took to destroy her utterly, during the time their treatment prolonged her life. Richard remained baffled, by his sick sister. Sick, as in morbid, macabre. He wrongly assumed a change of personality in her. Uncertain, confused, he spoke deliberately implying her presence in a distant future. Had she understood the prognosis? nobody knew. Because she confided in nobody except Ilario, and he talked to nobody but his wife. Awkward moments when Maxwell bit his tongue, choked in the middle of sentences, combined with Anna's studied ignorance of his domestic arrangement, created fresh tension in cold Richard. A vicious circle: Anna and Richard were very alike. It was not kind, it was cruel. Max tried to supply some gentleness. Anna let him hold her arm in the street, smiled at his small jokes. She rejected, carefully, the evidence of a sexual relationship: she knew homosexuality happened, she could see nightly how they slept in Richard's bed: she felt sure they did nothing in it. She believed what she preferred to believe: illness unterminal, sodomy improbable. Leave me room in which to hope. You must realise truth is unwelcome if forced upon me, forced into the open. I shall never publicly acknowledge loss of reasonable hope, and privately I hope even still now. Leave me space. Allow me a place in my mind where I may manoeuvre thoughts and notions freely. Alcohol? asked Richard, drawling. She passionately desired ginger beer. Yet it gave her wind. He registered distaste. Apologising pathetically, she wondered in brief despair: do I have to be so brave. Loving, hating him, her funny brother.

And not a soul supposes I consider suicide. Stiff and sore, Anna returns home, to the cottage, alone. Ilario away from home, at sea, really unwanted. He was aware his wife's courage denied conscious help, at least for a while she seemed happier organising a woman to do the housework, a man to fetch in wood. Recovering staunchly after a major operation, the beginning. At the beginning she refused to sit about moping. Once, she'd sworn to end her life in such a situation. She strolled along the river bank. Level ground suited the aches and pains. Driving taboo, the clutch being difficult. The compulsion towards suicide hardly fitted her character, the character other people recognised as Anna. But she loved, honoured, and admired the act. Admitted it to the code of her own strict morality. Therefore she had a sophisticated choice. And she intended to endure death as years ago she endured childhood. Neither death was natural, was to be natural. To protect her mind, to deflect the temptation to set a limit now, she compelled Ilario to treat her like a child, or a fool. She prescribed the best cure.

Steadfast, also, in solitude. Steadfast and so far secure. At this moment mesmerised not by water, by weed. Greenish weed to turn upon a body falling in and strangle it. The winter has almost gone, though the weather's icy. Primroses show yellow beside her path. Cowslips grow in the field. Bluebells deep in the woods. If only she could climb. She hears larks—she thinks she hears larks singing on the hill. Hares running over the hump of memory. Her throat felt thick. A lot of it was memory. She shivered. Resigned to decrepitude and numbness. To dead feet, to dead fingers. Did the physical numbness match a mental anguish. Keep walking. Keep walking, Anna. Keep right on to the end of the road. But the squelchy mud strained those torn muscles. Beeches elms ash trees elder bushes: and in memory firs silver birches yews heather hollies. Red berries. Is her preservation instinct, or does some quixotic whim of the human spirit maintain that rotten frame for nobler pleasures, sports, abstract pastimes: which is more intellectual: ceasing by one's own hand and will to exist or electing to accept the punishments of dying. Fortunate the man whose time can catastrophically be determined: a heart attack, a war: great gun in the sky take aim, take aim and fire: a flapping bird falls, flying (a wild duck, I am no seagull). Inexplicably one becomes converted: I who'd die rather than consult a doctor throughout healthy life, in death am reconciled to hospitals surgeons chemicals the knife and all bitter pills. Obstinately I've no desire either to abdicate my own last gory rites.

A CHANGE
BROUGHT ABOUT BY THE SEA

3

Wind high, sea running, blue and white the sky, there would be no suspicion of it, anything amiss or untoward, ship rolling, firm, secure, weather singing, all day long, coast distant, in sight, islands, Cuba, Haiti, vanishing, dipping into this cradle below lat 20°N of tropical storms hurricanes tornadoes water spouts sundry bounty from a volatile god: Ilario obsessed, bothered by whatever friction existed between them, captain, and his chief mate, the grizzly embittered old bear who spoke neither Italian nor English, not even French, who speaking in nods figures scowls and blinks contrived to reject language of every kind: Anna, serene, keeping the peace, yet exacerbating it. To the south, then, Puerto Rico.

Brown, she'd lain in Caribbean sun, nose peeling, eye aching, a delightful weariness; the slight breeze always offshore cools Anna, and her skull through thin hair was as nut baked as if she'd been bald. Trousers she wears, baggy khaki denims, a cowboy shirt bought in Houston, Texas, scarf knotted, knots flying. Rampaging around like a monkey: the gorilla.

Night falls abruptly soon after sunset, steady Atlantic swell ESE, ship groaning, easing, creaking, they eat alone, drop into bed, listening, sleep without remembering their dreams. At five thirty Ilario wakes, by some sixth sense, aware. He lies: tense. His wife snoring, talking, snores snuffles conversation chatty, it mingles, confusing. Movement much the same, mild pitching, broad, smooth, down at the head, throb, screw, and up, trembling, shaking, making good speed, holding her course? yes, in a calm and gentle sea, so what's wrong he isn't certain. No change, discernible from here. Ilario puts on clothes quickly. Anna, he leaves behind. In the wheelhouse the chief mate does not speak. The captain's soft shoes oil his feet, soundlessly he glides into darkness, only the door squeaks. The chief mate is surly. In silence they contemplate a dim horizon, and a sky. The idle quartermaster stirs: to him Ilario directs his smile.

Ilario retreated to the chartroom, sniffing.

I observe gospel truth writ plain upon the barograph. Pressure has fallen, quite a lot, during the night, during one recent hour of our night. I look at the log. It has been entered thus: 2300hrs 1012, 0200hrs 1007, 0400hrs 1002. 0500hrs 997. Or 5mbs in 60 minutes. Falling, still falling. Now 996, it's no mistake. Where has the wind gone. Shifted. Turned completely, from SSW to ENE, soon will arrive strongly on the port bow. And he drew, treating the mate to a doodle: a pretty picture of some anticlockwise arrows arranged around a circle. The lull before the storm. You fool, you incompetent imbecile.

They were too far south and through negligence the ample opportunities to alter course in time had slipped away.

By dead reckoning we are: and he pokes at the chart with a protractor: we should be: both men sudden, excitable, gabbling in their separate lingo. Ilario slapped the slide rule over the other's fingers. He strives for control. Those stubby fingers he hates. Truly anguished. We are sailing straight into a major depression. Who slept, you or I? And a new gyro course is set. But by daybreak a man must stand at the wheel.

Ilario inspected the ship, taking toll of his mate's inadequacy. She was not ready to tackle the violence which comes to her. Then he will wake his wife.

The question being to identify the violence. An unreported one. Hurricane Dorinda flattens Florida, advancing NW at 5 knots, while to the north Hurricane Evangeline huffs and puffs harmlessly west at 7 knots. Tropical Storm Frances grips the bump of Africa. NNS Washington forecasts niente. No Gwendolen, Guinevere, or Gladys. No G. But we stare eye to eye. Conjured into our existence. To play with us.

There's little time, little enough time. He felt afraid. The deck spun as the sea rose and the wind came stronger until its noise was quite spectacular. There also gathered an accompaniment of rattles and bangs: and it began to rain. Everything happened as he expected.

The men found it impossible to work while the ship made headway. To reach the hatches they had to cross open deck fore and aft.

So at dawn on the morning of 10th September 1967, Ilario hove to. It took all his nerve to do this. He lay broadside to the waves while the mate went crackers, supposing Ilario, his captain, mad. A sloppy ship meaning little cause for his concern, the mate desired nothing better than to bolt towards the delicate grey skyline, for he was yellow, and stupid.

Because the engines were silent, an uncanny quiet distorted a louder sound, the sea. The crew sensed panic. Anna's moon face peered from the wheelhouse at lilliputian seamen clad in orange oilskins, or at crabs crawling: the mate having vanished in a temper, her old man cracked the whip.

Ilario wished she could be spirited to landfall. He noticed a glittery expression: she adored the crisis, the whole situation. Not a clue did she have, la poverina, unreal in an unreal world. Addicted to unreal drama.

Below, in hatch no 3, brooded the immense and bilious green eye of a 108 ton transformer. The heavy lift. Nearly as dangerous as loose grain.

And in an after hold, a clutch of vast cylinders.

I order these secured. Secured again.

The bosun scratches his thick head, he wisely winks. The bosun and I know each other well. He works fast, he has a lifetime of experience at sea.

And the bosun hides his funk. His blue funk from the crew. Bravo. Good fellow. Ilario touches his shoulder.

Fear not: soon we shall plough on through our appalling conditions, trusting a stability we in reality don't possess. He smiles, loving his ship, and his wife, his wife and his ship: Ilario takes heart. The tops of the waves already sprinkled the bridge: it could hardly be mere spray. But he relaxed, eating a marmalade sandwich.

It is now 0830 hrs and Anna travels to the saloon for breakfast. The stewards look cheerful. A lot of crockery breaks, though the cloths on the tables are sopping. Bacon and eggs appear, a miracle: in the galley surely cooking oil has lethal properties. Coffee requires indefinite suspension in the air by the person drinking it: a pragmatic unity. She grips her knife and her fork between the knees. Leans an elbow on her plate. Sinks an apple in her lap. Anchors the god-given food of paradise. Coping was fun.

Companionways suddenly slewed completely horizontal. The ship dipped a wing into the sea. A hailstorm struck. And visibility closed to nil. More and more water, lifted higher and higher, hitting us. The foredeck was awash. Scum tore through the scuppers. Waves breaking over the fo'c'sle thudded, disintegrated, ran across the duck's feathers and returned to earth. Even the minimal rigging at the mizzen mast streamed like a girl's hair in a gale. Poor Sparks lost his favourite aerial from the funnel amidships. One could watch, and only watch, the huge sea staggering along: the great sea coming. The sea driven into troughs by the wind fights a deep ocean swell. The compass needle twirled impossibly: the quartermaster, sweating, juggled in vain to hold a true course.

Anna sat at Ilario's desk in their dayroom, where she'd hours ago stowed loose objects. Using perseverance and a cargo plan she checked the mate's arithmetic. Her head ached. She showed her husband on the bridge her figures.

At present: the ship is rolling, has been rolling forty five degrees to port. Less, slightly, to starboard. Our limit, according to me, says Anna, is fifty two. Seven degrees grace saving us from capsize. Do you realise: we might all be dead.

Her delight is evident. Ilario was amused.

He thinks her hilarious.

Together they are enjoying the trip. Perhaps.

Ah yes. Yes. Yes.

So the day wears on. Ilario wished for second sight: not to hope but to *know* the heavy lifts were behaving sensibly. The mate retired in hysterics with both keys to his medicine locker, having nervously broke down. Always on board was a gun, the master's pistol. Galloping imaginations invent an insane mate, a man at the end of his tether, gone berserk. However, at sensitive middle age, commanded by a child of twenty seven and a hag he hates, he suffers from shock, exhaustion: he's sick, quite unused to emotion. Unaccustomed to quarrelling.

At two in the afternoon, Anna caught her breath. The wind dropped, the sky cleared, a rainbow shone in a frame of brilliant blue. Waves battered gently, dully, against the ship's side. The waves had no crests. The ship sailed serenely though a pleasure pond.

The people in her stared, as if transported to a foreign land: can this strange calm place be the eye? it seems likely. The hurricane came on our journey, we have grown fond of one another. For a very long time we struggled to defend our safety. Thinking we were free. Delivered from evil.

Ilario grinned: we are fine, you silly, her winds will turn on our tail.

The silence was terrible.

Once in your lifetime, Anna, you will see such a phenomenon: but I have been here before.

And in the warm weather, mirages gave our eyes islands: the sea splintered into strips of darkness and light. She smelt violets, her own beloved flower. Ilario guesses: ten miles, the absolute centre.

Hand in hand, they walk on deck, unfasten the watertight doors to each hold: a single cylinder has stirred, strained its moorings: good, good.

Then squalls came from nowhere, clouds obscured the sky, the lids of the sun closed abruptly, the horizon collapsed in rain. The wind did twist, veering sou'westerly, and the swell too threatened at a new direction. They began to push a confident passage out of the cyclone.

Lo and behold, at 1600 hrs: the mate. Ilario glared. Anna laughed. By 1800 hrs improvements are manifold. The climate has recovered.

In the hard Atlantic sunshine, in a strong sea with a following wind, she worked diligently to restore some kind of tranquil truce: forcing Ilario to a hot meal, persuading him to leave a maniac on the bridge.

You realise there was no alternative.

THE PASSAGE OF A SOUL
AT DEATH INTO ANOTHER BODY

2

Something is wrong, as I pass from the corridor silently into her room. Anna lies on her back.

To be supine is to be disarranged. She must die on her side. One side or the other. She must at least try to approach death in this way.

Also she is rather uncovered. The sheet and the counterpane are wrinkled in the region of her abdomen, the lower portion of it. She looks hot. She will not be feeling actually hot. She confronts not death but the ceiling.

A yellow knee has been hooked from the bed. The whole leg is exposed. It is also bare.

The knee and the leg lie abandoned. She flings them about. Wide open. In the position for easiest penetration. Beneath hospital linen her sex doth gape.

When I push the knee it bounces. It seems unattached to the pelvis, and the hip joint waggles wildly. Anna's limb has come undone from the torso. Like a broken doll's. A long time ago the hair prolific fell out, perhaps that shine would appeal to my wife, it doesn't entice me further. Furniture polish was evidently spread over the lumpy numb stuff. She strokes her much too solid flesh. We both wish she would melt.

Anna followed him with her eyes, a glimmer of intelligence there. Come stai, tesoro? he asked the puzzled face gently, busy unwrapping his flowers.

But her hand, unusually expressive, gestures towards her nose, waving royally. I stare. Visibly, audibly, she sniffs. Carries the fingertips to the nose, frowning. And her eyes are wide, they are disapproving. Then she creases the brow while in her mind she is shaking her head. The arm makes an arcing motion, causing the slack skin of the elbow to contract and at the hand to slide across the knuckle. The shoulder remains entrenched in the grey pillow.

I am entertained. By the pantomime. Innocently amused.

Then, oh then I at last notice you have clutched the sheet as well, and where you've clutched your sheet it's dirty. The stains on the sheet may be pretty decorations but they and your nails are dirty. And you have been telling me quite plainly: it smells, it is wrong.

More, it was nasty.

Anna had put a paw between the legs and dabbled in her faeces. Anna always always used a flannel for these private places. Convinced direct contact was only polite for crude males obliged by nature of their anatomy to hold themselves to wee wee, poor things.

Nowhere can I find a nurse. I'm ready to wash the hand. A trifle pale, my gills.

Ilario took a wet cloth and prepared to clean his wife, Anna.

It cannot be absolved by water or by soap alone. It has seeped into the lines of the palm, it has mapped her fate in vivid orange. And once drawn under the nails, traces tend to stay, a reminder for ever.

Stai calma. Wait.

Yet she has obediently extended one finger bone after another, five on each hand. She senses the tepid water, the soap slithering, the talcum powder, the dry towel: he is bathing a baby. Satisfied she scents the air.

She had shit on her lip.

Hastily Ilario wiped the mouth. He pulled the lip and saw that inside all was agreeably pink. He sighed. Her nails needed cutting so he returned to work on her hands. The crutch he didn't think he could cope with.

A hothouse cultivation, her nails. Fast growers. Trimmed, they are washable.

Defeated by a female crutch, not for the first time, I tackle the other end, content to cut her toes. The feet are very dead, and very large. Hysterically, because I've left the feet unvisited recently, I wonder: could they be decomposed? Discovering her feet anew, I remember them rasping my bum. The horn, the blue ankles, the twisted growths I snip tenderly (in revulsion), they are just the same, they are actually enduring better than the rest of her. I feel fond of such feet that tucked in still rear up under the blanket, a couple of erect penises, terminal but brave.

The atmosphere was bad. The hospital locker held a stock of sweeter smells. He sprinkled eau de Cologne and opened the window a crack. A precipice to the street, a pathway to the clouds, Anna as yet untransported, patience was paramount without doubt. A forced waiting.

Ilario had a brainwave and dribbled icy cold eau de Cologne onto her forehead: he drew for a joke the sign of a cross. Anna grunted enthusiastically. Or could it have been a strong protest.

Eh?

She replied, groaning.

—Because one does talk to her, one does.

He has gone to fetch a vase for his flowers. He brings her mauve flowers. Irises. Blue roses imported in bud from some foreign country. And of course, of course, violets. Squeezed by silver paper, their fragility hurts him. The elastic bands grate, on his nerves, against his nerveless fingers (her bumbling fingers, his precise touch) and the bunches are too small for his surefire firmness. Perpetually, Ilario feels too big.

Vases live in the ward kitchen. The journey is an ordeal. Anna's neighbours are daunting objects for his compassion. One woman lies fenced with white cot railings to a high bed, snoring: **DANGER, RADIATION,** do not come within three feet of this patient for more than five seconds. Monstrously alone.

He shivers for no good reason.

Accosted by another husband, the mate of a pale vegetable next door to us, I struggle not to scream: may he inspect my girl? Discrepancies—between his brain-bleeding tumour-nourishing spouse and mine—interest him unduly. He ogles her. He tells me I'm the split image of mother. Miserably I smile. I loathe the wretched fellow. Our cases are the elite, removed to eliminate distress in the main ward to cells private and particular: accordingly neither he nor I see the women and the men who will recover, if any here will, except on voyages for flower vases.

Anna shouted: in in in.

The words rise to the surface, flotsam of her mind. It has all to rhyme, causing strange satisfaction. And oh how bitterly I realise the true significance of a second childhood.

She follows thought trails so faint and confusing in their pictures that she can only repeat what she sees on the eye of her brain.

Morsels from a once important vocabulary she eats, chewing them over with relish.

But the prize enigmatically eludes her. Singing out her anxieties, perplexities, her anguish.

It was a song, of which the conclusion never came.

I held the twitching hand. It responded, gripping me in a most friendly fashion.

She looks dumb: she is extremely noisy.

Nurse arrives banging the door blind. Anna jumps. The loudest sounds penetrate.

The nurse is a child starched.

We discuss Anna's conversation. I cannot explain. It is not to be admitted. This solemn infant understands more than I probably guess. Was Anna calling my name? she asks. I say, no. The name of your son. No no.

My English difficult, I indicate the sheet. She nods, peers brusquely beneath. She pulls back the bedclothes. The cheeks of Anna's bottom are sympathetically slapped. Anna isn't permitted resentment. The cheeks of Anna's bottom are separated: Anna isn't permitted shame. There seems hardly any recognisable bottom remaining to her anyhow. The flesh has wasted away. The bones on their own don't strike me as quite *right*. My little nurse clucks, mildly shocked, pretending drama for me; and she drops the flap of that awful bottom having grasped the full extent of its mess.

I shall be banished when she returns presently. They will usher me into the ceremonious corridor.

The time since Anna last walked and talked is interminable, ending where she began, among twenty similarly sad females. Then flowers were the only things of beauty I could bring and joy was strictly limited.

She knew what to do without being told. If the speech could not be clear, the mind at least was lucid. So Anna practised her reading, writing, and arithmetic very diligently.

She counted the coins in her purse.

She copied laborious names, and addresses.

Every day she paid, from the coins in her purse, for *The Times* to be delivered to her bed. She imagined she read it, she imagined what she read in it, fluently she read aloud: no such graphic revelations were printed in the paper. She had created a brilliant and deeply unconscious pretence.

But the menu she dealt with unerringly, in the tiniest duplicated type. Intent on her fat free diet: eating it preserved her identity. She really did read the menu, and made crosses in boxes opposite breakfasts dinners suppers two days ahead.

At the top of her voice, she talked, often about suppositories. She criticised me, saying: tell me stories. Her brain was bursting with energy, with the thrill of learning. I felt unequal to it, to her, and unequal simply. In her sketch book she drew many wobbly vases of flowers, the still life around her.

Who are you? Anna asked Ilario. Who am I?

At this moment manhandled, things are horrible for her. She scolds them. They must tug at her legs, and tidy her. I listen in my corridor, bereaved. It is dreadful.

Anna fell silent.

They crept out shutting him inside.

He bent over her: she was awake. He took a rose from the vase. With the blue rose bud he tapped her nostrils. And she sniffed.

Delighted, he exhausted her, demanding these sniffs again and again and again.

He has communicated using a flower.

Nearby someone else is screaming.

THE STATE OF TIME
OF BEING A CHILD

3

I, a child.

The fox leaves a dense covert for the open plough.

Gipsies camp in our lane, tethering three ponies.

The voice of the huntsman sings down the valley.

Listen: branches crackle, his horse tramples dead bracken, delicately treads rabbit trails through the furze, or stands stock still in a ride: straining our ears, pricking our ears to the small distant sound of his horn: and waiting, sharp groundfrost fades in bright sunlight across the steep hill. Anna has a pony of her very own, she is eight. Jackson takes Anna on a leading rein to the meet. People on tall horses say good morning, it is supremely necessary to mumble a reply. Her hair squirms in a net at the nape of her neck. The groom taught the little girl to ride. Brutal but successful. A nice seat essential. Anna and the pony part company often. All part of life. Jackson wears ratcatchers for hunting, his pepper and salt, his shiny gaiters job. Last night he cleaned the tack specially by the harness room fire, sipping laced cocoa. Goodness, what roses in your cheeks. Jackson's are indeed ruddy. However, the gentleman in pink spoke to me. My gloves slither on the damp reins. Reins lathered in sweat. A fine scenting morning: and Jackson touches his cap. Master will draw Fiddler's kale. I fancy a lean vixen sleeps amongst that dark wavy cabbage. An almighty crack: Dauntless, Rambler, Regal. At home in the larder hang rows of clotted nostrils. Shall Anna abandon her pony, shout, scream, bellow? Purple hens, pheasants till they drop, hares gnawed internally by maggots. Late, eh: Jackson fumbles for his watch. Calves are shot, cows slaughtered, cats sent to heaven: those whom the gods love. Chin up, he hisses. Pale white women in masks of powder and cream conceal searing smiles on scarlet lips behind veils. D'you mark, tis the dog pack? Puce bloodshot men champ jolly foaming jaws. Ho ho, Miss Anna, chin up. A hideous collective apoplexy. How blue, blue was the sky. We'd only be wise to find a cart track handy. The cautious groom removes his charge from the fray. Presently, a hundred horses bustle past us, splashing. At one discreet green corner, silence falls. Loud conversation dies, as hounds pour endlessly into the kale. Birds warble, soil crumbles, a kicker humps the red ribbon on his chestnut tail. The field freezes. Steamy, our breath. Drawing a blank. Cunning bugger, thik poultry stealer. To the plantation, then. Jackson sets a child's pace: he and I arrive sedate, unruffled for the long, long wait. But: do you hear a quaver: a single hound speaks again: the moment of complete quiet: the pack in full cry: not a soul stirs. A holloa, and Anna tingles deliciously: in the deepest bit of her body something snaps. She has this unbearable pleasure. Far yonder vanishes a tiny figure at covert point intent: the fox slips over the wide black earth: music echoes round the hollow trees: he is blowing his horn, gone away: gone away: sound approaches and retreats: out of the edge of the wood hounds come, flickering. Gather your reins, Miss Anna. A jolting, gasping gallop: we skirt a bullfinch: I've got a stitch: Jackson: you're an awkward passenger: Jackson: is he deaf:

she licks the mud from her lips: stifles a scream, I'm falling: pay attention: but she tumbles, lies flat, and winded: well, he took a tiny stream, you didn't: spitting crushed grass: his large raw hands: in the sky huge clouds: I want to seem braver than actually I am: gittup, grunts Jackson, I'm proud of you. Hounds have checked and the fainthearts bolted home. She eats her sandwiches slumped in the saddle. Delirious. The earths are stopped: she's a vixen: a white tip to her brush. Had enough? No. Imagination leaps the moon. Too much trotting on the hard high road. A brisk canter: the field dwindles: some people become lost, or lame. Jackson has saved me for the kill. Although he dislikes my parents the Master shakes me by the hand tips up my chin as if to kiss me and dabs my cheeks with a bleeding stump. Oh tears of anguish, exhaustion. Anna clutched the prize possession, it dripped down her breeches. A very great honour: a little girl.

THE CARRYING OF A PERSON
TO ANOTHER PLACE OR SPHERE
OF EXISTENCE

4

And still she is staring into the flames, always staring into fire, the flames of eternal damnation dry stiff the tears on her yellow chalk cheeks.

My poor wife alone, without me, although I am very near. We are separated, prised apart. There was no help for it, no help for her.

Shall you carry also me to your grave, inevitably: a future destruction.

The silence between us has been total.

The greatest longing, unimaginable desires, to have, once more to hold, to sit beside a person dying, to comfort, to walk in that valley: the shepherd but another paltry human spirit, inadequate. The occasion demands superhuman strength and my staff has withered within you. Your cunt stuck like a pig's throat drenches our earthland in blood, pulsing torrents of it: and still, still the heart beats.

I long to go out again into the land of the living. You imprison me in an armchair opposite your grief, a cosy armchair being not my milieu.

Anna watches astronauts stomping around the moon, wondrous television: I imagine, she says, myself on the moon. And I watch *her*, unable to avoid her, alive to each gesture, to every thought in her head. Raw, I perceive. My awareness is stripped naked, then flayed.

I imagine, she says, all sorts of things—sums, pictures, symbols—and my imagination contains, at random, descriptions made by those whose creative vision was infinitely grander than mine own. I can imagine what I do not understand if some other one affirms knowledge of it and given that this was beyond my own experience, capacity. Death *is* lived through: simply none survives to tell the tale.

The brain plays tricks on her. She's afraid of losing control, supposing she did have control—certainly she valued it—over the myths in our minds. The child builds sandcastles in order to destroy them: let it be realised our constructions are there to climb.

And though the earth's centre would seem an ideal womb heaven, we keep the skies reserved for heaven—it will stay aloft above us for ever: thus our unconscious concept of gravity. Or does some special heaven lie for Anna under the sea.

How pleasant it is in the sun, observes my wife now, dispassionately.

I must remain not in heaven but in our house. Surrounded and bounded by infancy, regressing too into a world of shit and piss. I have to lend an ear: these are her troubles: I shall listen without disgust.

I am eaten by my guilt. My wholesomeness offends us both, my undamaged body arranged in a position of patient waiting, vulturous. Divided by a few feet and consciousness.

Anna seen objectively isn't a pretty sight. She possesses an inner unserenity. She fights, is fighting. The jowls hang aggressively from the extremities of her skull. She touches her jaw unaccustomed to such exacerbated thinness.

And I have grown to hate—one ends by hating—the

person, the object of my love. I want to swear: I love you dearest Anna. Yet I require you to die. I dread much more of this. I shall be free if you do die. And if I consider killing you it is to release me rather than you.

Should she be put out of her misery? Is suffering necessary? Does my wife grow nobler through bearing pain? Humiliating pain.

Or may I execute my sorrow. See, it is I who am ill-equipped. She sails on, holding her womb before her like a spinnaker. While I am only anchored to her ribs.

She almost enjoys the challenge. But I, Ilario, always the spear-carrier, do tremble transfixed in her limelight.

Distortions balloon in my mind, the victim's purged because I swallow constantly our emetic. I could wring her throat until the face turns purple as a turkey.

I examine and I memorise her, wondering if the memory will become more real to me than the reality. Treasured memory, my gift. Played repeatedly, beloved recall. A continuation of things present. The flexible furniture of my life. Memory living—in living memory. A deck of cards dealt in spontaneous sequences. Shall I love her so intensely in ten years. Or my own self die?

Textures press against my eyes, small lines run across her lips: I am a microscope.

I squeeze her. Brains spill, are strewn about the room. I lick at her ears, lapping up her thoughts. She tastes nice, human; the taste of these brains is the taste of her cunt. The female has been hung from the ankles. It all trickles out for my frantic tongue.

No no no. Gently I stroke the furry cheeks, kiss her mouth without opening it, clutch the stubbly grey hair in my fingers, dry the slobber from her slack drooling face the way a mother cat might her young. I drape her arms around me, I force her to smile, or myself to smile. The pulse at the throat beats, is still.

At least upon our bed we should be free from constraint. Would you pile yourself over me, weak Anna, trying to remember the construction of love making?

Your hand, so nearly a ghost, tantalises unbearably. Exquisite! Pierce my lips with the bristles of your chin. And my nostrils distend in the stink of your putrefaction. You cry, make me well, Ilario, kiss me better. Or silent, she's too proud to utter.

Impotent we are, the two of us, to cure. I fuck fluidly and frequently to no avail. Sperm has no *permanent* healing power. It merely illuminates her expression for an hour, a minute, a second.

And we sit nailed to our chairs here, one of us thinking about the other, one of us just thinking.

Under stony black trousers exist pallid legs to fondle. Gnarled, her legs. Belonging nevertheless to me. Swamped in coddling clothes will be some bare breasts. Concealed in the belly, cancer sprouts. Tenderness overwhelms.

If I lifted you bodily—god knows you are light enough—from your chair, could you separate the legs or are they stuck with glue together? May we dab at each other's bones with bones dressed for decency in earthly flesh (yours whitest, mine brownest) like darting fishes in a tank, a tactile performance? If I carry you, transport you up the stairs, will you straighten your knees and allow me between them, or are you already stiffening into a daylight corpse? Is it easier if I roll you out, my pastry, on the glowing carpet where the fireheat excites you. *Puff* pastry, Anna. Shall we exert ourselves with sweat and semen to the smell of burnt applewood and the sound of hissing, little pops, and baby noises (the sap rising). Please: can't you touch *me*?

No answer. The static gloom appalls him.

Perhaps it's *that* I need to murder, my penis a thousand pins, not stuffing but pricking, to galvanise a sick girl. Enraged, I'll masturbate, providing sacred anointment to smear on your bald head.

The womb I see hath a foul face, glimmers evilly at me, winks, pouts, frowns: copulation grows nightmarish: I flatten my stomach over the fangs of obscenity. This is madness.

Aching for a familiar response, I grovel when, disfigured herself, she exclaims: you're gross. Eyeing the contamination. Not her tumour. The husband. Me.

Stationed in a sitting position, I visualise those trousers off. I imagine kneeling below her: a kind of worship: and a figure naked from the waist *down* sitting in an armchair seems erotic, extravagantly so—a weird normality. The torso dissolves into two faces, neither of which smiles. Two noses, two mouths, four lips. And the slow painful eye regarding me invisibly changes. I offer a portion of the fire.

Her lashes dampen my absurdly soft own cheeks. You will cry eventually. Her two eyes flash wide, the red gorge gapes, suddenly I'm a bird, laden with a worm. She sags towards me.

You fumble with my foreskin, preferring a ripe banana from the kitchen.

I feel the brittle nails. She fiddles peaceably.

Oh oh, her crutch has lost all its hair, she is an infant there.

One doesn't fuck children.

I close her legs. She moans, rocks in my arms instead. Tiny gasps escape the lungs. How, how to soothe you, Anna.

I place my face against your face in a gesture of complete surrender. Aren't we beginning, then, a love unsexual, a forgotten loving, almost unreal to grown people.

Anna looks not at me. The window panes capture the heron flying along the river. That is where the water is. She wanted, I know, to founder at sea, to drown: a foolish child's fancy. She was unaware of how terrible a death drowning can be. I never told her: this strange affinity with water is a fearless notion no true seaman holds. Should I have thrown you overboard at the end of our last voyage together? Must I wave goodbye to my wife as she sinks to the sea bed? The ecstasy is yours, love, and I cannot make it mine.

The skin of her neck was a goose's, plucked and puckered. Her chest, the wishbone cavity, fluttered. A chin dug into my shoulder; it was the horse's jaw. Through her teeth flowed crocodile tears. Her breathing, a bad egg. Unspoken words trembled in our hands, quietly we kissed, and we embraced one another.

TIME THAT IS TO BE
OR COME HEREAFTER

3

Ilario has his tanker. He takes her, like a toy, around the world. She's the true iron maiden, *ms original sin*, another virgin for him: brand new untried, not yet ridden: a hulking great creature of unbelievable stiffness and unmanoeuvrability—in the worst weather placid, unruffled—and about as attractive as some grotesque sausage. Speed being her peculiar quality he loves her: there is a splendour in charging across oceans at a gallop faster than the wind.

So finally will come the fog, in one perfect last metaphor. He is in fog, real fog: a thick pea souper. He's green with fear, short of sleep (world weary), very neurotic: careful, most terribly careful. Hawking his vast tonnage of crude oil along our coastline and its miles of pretty bathing beaches, bays, and creeks. Inshore, summer bank holiday seems in sight, at sea nothing. Not even the lighthouses which surround him—Start Point, Eddystone, Wolf Rock. All watching, waiting to prop his failing courage up. Our position, to observe. His, the pursuit of madness. He cannot forget his Anna. It is all engraved on the memory. Radar in constant turmoil—lumps of land quiver, illuminated briefly, vanish into their own secret and everlasting night. Earth and water defined by unreliable magic. A fog so dark merely to have the eye naked was to appear quite blind. Bountiful the radio bleeps: uttering repeated identification. Memory, a tortoise shell. Is Ilario any less a person, lacking possessions to bleed emotion? Never mind, she will bleed enough for two, for both of us, rupturing her guts on the rocks of foolish error. A lifetime's nervous exhaustion spewed over the dim receding sea.

THE PASSAGE OF A SOUL
AT DEATH INTO ANOTHER BODY

3

absolution: a dismissal

Anna lies there, looking very small. A child again, bab-bling of heaven. So the humiliation belongs not to flesh alone.

He has never felt closer to her.

Perhaps only one person remains in this sickly room.

Then he hears the death rattle. A sound of utmost poi-gnancy. It drags at her throat. It is quite peaceful.

Poor man.

The woman, whom the man loved, longs to die: but I do not know what I cannot imagine. Her last clear idea.

It is finished, it is not finished, the moment never comes, this bitter taste in my mouth can be the only end.

OTHER NEW YORK REVIEW CLASSICS

For a complete list of titles, visit www.nyrb.com.